HOPEFULLY EVER AFTER

James Webster

Published by Inspired Quill: April 2025

First Edition

This is a work of fiction. Names, characters and incidents are the product of the author's imagination. Any resemblance to actual events or persons, living or dead, is entirely coincidental. The publisher has no control over, and is not responsible for, any third-party websites or their contents.

Content Warning: This title contains mention of assault, classism, death (parental, partner), mental illness, police brutality and war.

Contact the author through their website: https://strangelittlestories.tumblr.com

Chief Editor: Sara-Jayne Slack
Proofreaders: Clare Stevens, Mara Liddle & Tom Grover
Cover Design: ChocolateRaisinFury
Typeset in Minion Pro

Paperback ISBN: 978-1-913117-29-0
eBook ISBN: 978-1-913117-30-6
Print Edition

Printed in the United Kingdom
1 2 3 4 5 6 7 8 9 10

Inspired Quill Publishing, UK
Business Reg. No. 7592847
https://www.inspired-quill.com

Praise for James Webster

“*Funny, thought-provoking, heartbreaking, empowering, unique, and utterly wonderful,* Heroine Chic *contains every story I wish I’d heard as a little girl told in fairy-tale format. Witches, fairies, scientists, librarians, queens, superheroines, there’s something in each of these stories for everyone. From quiet little girls who make friends with monsters, to new twists on old and familiar faces, this is going to stay with you for a long, long time.*”

–RK Summers,
author of *The Old Ways*

“*At each page, I feel that tremulous bubbling sense of fitness, of wonder, that I remember having on reading Calvino’s* Invisible Cities *or Carter’s* Bloody Chamber *for the first time. This book is delicious.*”

–Antonia GR,
reviewer

“*Every part of this book is still relevant, still deep, and still jaw-droppingly beautiful.*”

–I. Slipper,
reviewer

“*If you’re not a short story reader but would like to be, if you love viewing humanity, love and power through new (broad, inclusive and supportive) lenses and if you are looking for something that nurtures your soul and is somehow so much bigger than the sum of its parts, then this is for you!*”

–S. Opaque,
reviewer

For Ayrton.

Because hope should be more than patience with a hat on.

Table of Contents

1. Away From Home.. 1

2. White Light 5

3. Blank Slate 9

4. Bright 11

5. Crucible 15

6. No Words... 19

7. By your fingernails 21

8. Specks... 23

9. Sunday Club 25

10. The Blessings Maker 29

11. Salt Heart 33

12. Downpour 39

13. Raindrops 43

14. Favours 45

15. In which you invite the evil fairy to your wedding.......... 49

16. Your Story 53

17. Be Gay, Do Crime(s).. 57

18. Beehives 59

19. Falling Stars... 63

20. Watered 67

21. Peaches 71

22. New Wings.. 73

23. Grazed Knees 77

24. Right.. 83

25. Snow Angel 87

26. Eat This Poem... 89

27. The Brave Little Owl.. 93

28. Thistle 99

29. When I Found My Wings 105

30. Distance 109

31. Heart Jumper 111

32. Ladder 113

33. Missives 119

34. Your Call Is Important 121

35. Forlorn Hope 127

36. Maybe 131

37. Once Upon A Time 135

38. The Longest Night 137

39. The Milk and Honey of Human Kindness 139

40. A Love Song For Friendships Past 143

41. Someone To Watch Over Me 145

42. The Void Winks 149

43. A Wizard Did It 151

44. Sometimes A Wild Dream 155

45. The Queen and the Goblin 159

46. Home 161

47. Winter 165

48. The Salt Anniversary 167

49. Tough 173

50. Toothbrush 177

51. Seed Energy 181

52. Where The Light Gets Out 185

Dear Reader.. 191

Acknowledgements.. 193

About the Author 197

More From This Author 199

1.

Away From Home

THE FIRST TIME the band of survivors stopped to rest, they were somewhat surprised to see Suzy nailing a painting up on the charred wallpaper. Most of the buildings in that village were burned out wrecks, but they'd found one that still had walls and most of a roof. It was enough, at least, to allow them to attempt sleep without the fear of being out in the open, and with a thin barrier between them and the oppressive gloom of the ever-twilight.

Most of the group weren't sure what to make of Suzy's efforts. You would think, in dark times like these, that everyone would have their eccentricities. But the thing about hard times is: they tend to weed out any idiosyncrasies that don't *help you survive*.

One member of the group piped up, in a voice more bemused than critical.

"Uh, we're only going to be here for the night – well, for one *sleep*, you know…"

Suzy just smiled and made sure the painting was hanging straight.

She repeated this odd process at every shelter they found along the way.

And the group would quickly learn that this was not Suzy's only strange habit.

For one, her bag was usually full of assorted luxuries like rugs and ornaments and art supplies, rather than the food and weapons most of the group prized. Even the group's traders and tinkerers found her collection odd – so little of it had any barter value or could make anything practical.

Oh sure, she was good at whittling a wooden stake. As good as anyone. But she could more often be found applying her skills to reclaimed furniture.

And if a Leech tried to feed on them? Well then they were glad to have her on side, for she was as fierce as sunlight. But that wild fury was nothing compared to the vibrant, abstract, and violently beautiful paintings that she'd leave on the walls of their shelters.

"Why does she do this?" A small group asked Gerald, the man who had known her longest. "Isn't it a bit of a liability?"

Gerald smiled warmly. "Oh, sure, it seemed that way to me at first, too … but have you ever noticed?"

"Noticed what?"

"We don't get attacked when we rest." Gerald gestured to the broken walls around them. "I've been with Suzy through a few groups like this, who all did things differently, and one thing is the same between all of them: if Suzy is with us, then whatever shelter we choose is safe."

"You mean…?"

"Yep. That's her particular kind of magic." Gerald

chuckled. "She makes a house a home. Enough to keep Leeches out."

The survivors looked around them. They had to admit, the drapes and rug complemented each other beautifully.

Suzy said nothing as she finished off her latest mural, beautifully illuminated by a homemade lamp.

And the half-lit world was a little brighter.

2.

White Light

WHEN JEMMA SAW the big white light, she knew immediately what it was.

And that's why she started running the other way.

She emerged back into her body, gasping and shaking. Not that either behaviour did her any good, given her body no longer needed to breathe, and a bit of shaking was doing nothing to get her out of the coffin.

Indeed, for a considerable amount of time, it did not seem like she *would* get out of the coffin. For the weight of earth above her was crushing, and her stubborn reanimation had sadly failed to imbue her with any kind of supernatural strength.

But over the course of days, she felt as if she wore her fists to stubs as she pummelled the coffin lid to splinters.

Over the next week, she struggled up through the earth and felt the rough dirt strip the dry skin from her face.

She had been in fairly good nick when they buried her. But by the time she arose, she looked every inch the creature from beyond the grave.

And once she emerged, she looked around her, enjoyed a brief redundant breath, and tutted at the world in general.

Then she set to work – for she was likely to be on this planet for a very long time, and she was determined to care for it as if it were her own child. Indeed, after a few generations of fighting, campaigning and generally getting her claws into the clay of the world, you could certainly consider it to be, in some small way, her progeny.

MANY HUNDRED YEARS later, she sits in an armchair. It is as comfortable as anything is these days, given she has little left in the way of flesh to cushion herself.

"I suppose I only really have one question…" The interviewer says, idly drawing complex 3D doodles through their holo-pad. "How do you do it? When your body's breaking down, how do you keep going? When everyone around you calls you a monster, how do you forgive them? When every generation repeats the mistakes of the last, how do you not despair? Forgive my bluntness but… why the hell haven't you given up on us yet?"

Jemma pulls back the remains of her upper lip, revealing a rictus that could be generously described as a smile.

"Did I ever tell you what I saw when I died?"

"A great white light, wasn't it?"

"There was… a little more to it than that." Jemma no longer has eyelids worth closing, but her eyeballs slide back in her head and you can tell they weren't seeing anything in this world. "First of all, it's important to remember that dying sucks. It *hurts*. And it's terrifying. And you will never feel so alone. But after that… yeah, it was a great, bright, white city. A gleaming white world. Full of shining, perfect people. I can still see them smile, and to know that smile was to know bliss. And I carry a little piece of that white light with me now."

Her eyes swivel wildly before fixing unsettlingly back on the interviewer.

"And it makes me *so* fucking angry."

"Angry?" The interviewer blurts out the word in a disbelieving snort.

"Can you picture it? A perfect world just on the other side of this one. And we don't get to see it until we die? What the ever-loving flangepuppets?" It surprises the interviewer that the text-to-speech software even recognises that last word. "Whenever I start to doubt, I just think of that great white light. Because I'll be damned – and I mean that quite literally – *damned* if the only perfect world I get to see will be one I had to die to get to. That version of reality is *unacceptable* to me. And I plan to cling on until the world matches my expectations."

"So… it's stubbornness then?" says the interviewer, not wanting to use a word quite as damning as 'rage' or 'delusion'.

"Stubbornness? Oh no." Jemma makes a wet sound through her ragged neck that's the closest she can manage to laughter. "It's hope."

3.

Blank Slate

T HE PROBLEM WITH the Blank Slate(tm) is that it's a misnomer.

Sure, on the surface it seems perfect. A couple who are having problems inscribe them on the slate's shimmering surface and then wipe them away. Hey presto, away with all those pesky betrayals and indiscretions. Or, when you decide it's time to part, you just write each other's names and move on, baggage free.

But it rarely works out that way. The same problems inevitably resurface. Couples who had forgotten each other inexplicably find themselves railroaded into each others' lives, despite the best efforts of their mutual friends to prevent those particular trains from wrecking again. We call it the 'Eternal Sunshine' effect.

You see, despite the best efforts of the field's leading psycholomancers and warlocks of Psyche, true memory erasure is still beyond us. Perhaps it always will be. The mind is resilient and its programming runs deep. The subconscious has backups we can't access and will almost always attempt to restore the lost data.

Why do you think we're so careful using the blasted slates in medical environments? Trust me, the last thing you want is a trauma victim beginning to exhibit symptoms without any memory of the traumatic events.

So why do we still use them?

Well, for that I need to tell you a story.

I was performing an analysis on a unit returned by a couple who *kept* erasing each other and getting back together. I ran every divination and diagnostic I knew and couldn't find a thing wrong with it. In desperation, I cracked it open.

Every wipe was preserved there, scored into densely packed layers of slate, like fossils in the earth or the life rings of a tree. It was beautiful. It refused to wipe anything at all – it was a backup. An external hard drive for their pain.

I probably shouldn't have read it, but I couldn't help myself. Their lives read like soap operas. Most fascinating of all was this: in each iteration of their relationship they remembered the lessons of the last. They were slightly kinder to each other. Their breakup more harmonious. Their feelings less frayed. The script of their imperfect lives that much closer to perfect.

I'm trying to convince HQ to rebrand the Slate as The Palimpsest: storing your pain until you're ready for it.

4.

Bright

"I AM GOING to devour you," said the voice from the darkness. "But before I do, tell me your name. For I like to know the names of all those brave enough to enter my Labyrinth."

"My name is Lucy," said Lucy, keeping very still. In the breath after she had spoken, she could feel the eddies her words had made in the stale air as they traced patterns across her skin.

"You are brave, Lucy," said the voice of what she could only assume was the Minotaur.

"Not brave," she said. "Bright."

"In a short while – for you only have a short while left – I believe you will reconsider how bright it was to get lost in my maze…"

She could smell the monster's breath. It was rank, but also sweet. The way decay always was. Around the edges, the honey rot was cut with the reek of sweat layered over the musk of fur. She could feel the heat in the air that told her the creature was very close indeed. Part of her brain was screaming. She took a breath.

"Did you know that Lucy comes from the Latin 'Lucius'?"

The presence in the darkness faltered. The pattern of its breathing changed ever so slightly. A little less predator and a bit more presence.

"I don't really see the relevance, my little lunch-meat."

"Okay," her voice was perfectly even as she turned the words over carefully in her mouth to soften them, "but if you hear me out, I think you'll see where I'm coming from. Okay?"

The Minotaur laughed a short, choked laugh. Lucy felt it wash over her cheek in hot rancid exhalations.

"You have until you cease to amuse me…"

"No." The full stop was sharpened to a point on her teeth. It hit the Minotaur like an arrowhead. "I want you to take this seriously. They might be my last words, after all."

A very long pause followed. It felt like forever, but she remained patient.

"Go on," said the creature.

"From the Latin: 'Lucius'. Meaning 'as of light'. I believe that words have power. That they do not just describe the things they signify, but *shape* them. So do you know why a being of light – why a woman as bright as me – would get lost in a Labyrinth?"

"To get eaten?"

Lucy smiled. Exhaled. As she did, the labyrinth slowly began to fill with gentle luminescence.

Lucy looked out with wide, knowing eyes and saw the

Minotaur shrinking back from the brightness that rolled in waves off of her skin.

"Because she knew she wasn't the only woman trapped there."

She held out her hand to the Minotaur. The creature stared at her as if it had never seen something so frightening.

"The king imprisoned you down here just as surely as he did me," Lucy continued. "At least I knew what I was getting into. I can only imagine how hard this has been for *you*. Still, I probably shouldn't be too shocked. Kings have always been the enemy of powerful women like us."

They stood there, Lucy and the Minotaur, with one hand outstretched and nothing but stale air and fear separating them.

And Lucy waited, patiently, for the Minotaur to take her hand.

5.

Crucible

I N THE MUTABLE World, at the apex of the Wars of the Real, two men met in the Crucible of All Things.

This place had not existed a few days earlier. It would not exist the next dawn. But – for a brief time only – this was the most important place in existence. This was the spot where any choices would echo and ripple, transmuting the world to match its shape.

Did the two men meet there because it was so important? Or did the place become important because the two men would meet there? Who can say. All I can say is what happened.

The men approached the Crucible. One came from the east. One came from the north.

The one who approached from the east was an old soul, though he did not look it; his face was youthful, his eyes bright, his smile as easy as a breeze carrying the first scent of spring. But if you were around him for any length of time, you would know it. Nothing he did in particular would give it away – his every gesture was welcoming, his every utterance thoughtful and light.

It was just a vibe. A sense that some part of this man had *seen some shit*.

The one who approached from the north was a goblin. Or, to put it more accurately, one of the fair folk. His was a history of great and beautiful and terrible things – all the joys of endless summer and all the power of sudden storms. This being of noble grace and glory, who could have chosen any form, just so happened to prefer a more feral shape.

But you would know, as soon as you saw his grin, that this was a creature who had crawled happily out of a thicket of thorns. Who had stepped, whole and fully formed, from a vine of ripe grapes.

Yes, it would be more accurate to call him fair. But it would be more truthful to call him *goblin*.

The two walked, at no great rush, towards the Crucible. One at a steady and even pace, one swaggering.

They came to the centre of this locus of possibility, where a world breaking under its own weight could be made whole or sundered entirely, and they regarded each other for a moment.

"I've come to make things better," said the Old Soul.

Behind his words, you could feel a history – of strange sights and weary roads. Here was a person who had travelled the changing lands and had decided to stay in them. To stop, where he could, and to linger a while and help. A person who saw places and people with needs, and realised in that moment that he was a person with ability. It was only natural that he would do what he could.

"I've come to make things *worse*," said the Goblin.

And his words were alive with mischief and deep with fatigue. It is so very tiring, after all, to have a good time for such a *long time*. This being knew wildness, knew madness, and knew ecstacy, and found beauty and kindness in all of them. He had made it his life's endeavour to help others to do the same. He was a person who had seen all the forgotten corners of the new world and the old and had carefully mapped the fractures that shot through them – who had mapped the world in its breaking and raged against them as much as he loved them.

A moment followed where the air around them stretched with tension, ready to snap. It was the kind of moment where only two things could happen:

One, they would kill each other. The heavy air would break with thunder and these two beings – these two men who carried a world's potential in their shadows – would wreck themselves against each other.

Or two … what *actually* happened.

The Old Soul looked the Goblin up and down and saw all there was to see, then bit his lip and carefully said, "Well … I suppose we could do both. If you'd like."

The Goblin stared back with goblet-wide eyes and grinned his grin that was like a crack in the void.

"Yeah. That sounds good. Let's do it… together."

And the two men walked back out of that place of change and brought it back into the world, side by side.

They made it better. They made it worse. It was beautiful.

6.

No Words

FOR SIX NIGHTS now, Briar Rose had been struggling to sleep. She kept dreaming of dragons.

Prince Philip had tried talking to her about it, but he had always been a person for action, not words. Perhaps it was not his fault; perhaps the words simply didn't exist.

So, on the seventh night, he took a handful of hairs from her head and, while she tossed and turned, he went to work outside.

In the morning, Briar thought her eyes deceived her, for the entire courtyard around the castle was filled with flowers.

"What?" This wasn't like any hallucination she'd had before.

"Do you like them?" Philip handed her a steaming mug.

She breathed the steam in deep.

"You planted roses for me?"

"Not roses." Philip smiled and carefully moved one of the flowers to the side. "Thorns."

"I don't understand."

The thorns glinted like stars in the morning dew.

"They grew in the night." He leaned into her and he smelled of soil and blood. "I'm glad you managed to get a little sleep."

"Well, this is nice to wake up to…"

She knelt down by the nearest bush and breathed in the scent of roses.

"I didn't have any words. But I had seeds. I hope they can bring you some peace."

She tested her finger against one of the thorns and bit her lip as it pierced her skin.

"I'm not sure thorns will keep the dragons away…"

"No, but perhaps you can."

"How so?"

"Each plant has one of your hairs wrapped in the roots. As you sleep, your magic will make them grow and rise up. They're not a wall or a cage."

Static crackled on her skin. And she blew smoke out of her nose.

"These will be *my* dragons."

Briar Rose managed only scant sleep that night.

And Philip never did find the right words.

But everyone agreed, in the few hours that Briar did manage to rest, that the flight of rose dragons over the castle was quite beautiful.

7.

By your fingernails

When you have fallen so far
You are looking up at the gutter
And no longer believe in stars

Cling on by your fingernails

When the world is all edges,
Intricate gears, sharpening infinitely
When it's too much, too big, too messy

Dig your nails into the edifice
And squeeze till it becomes a wish

Your fingers are stronger than you think
There is gristle in your palms
Your claws will regrow if you wreck them

Cling. Cling. Sink them in. Cling on.

There may be time later to puzzle out
How you got to this blank chess board

And play your pawn self back 'cross the void

But for now – gouge a bloody bolthole and cling.

Heed not the tide-washed voice
Telling you to let go of the one rock
That still glistens to you

That is the part of you who listened
To the petty tyranny of eyeless cogs
That never saw a place for you.

It's not their fault
They paid attention
But how heartbreaking to know
The loudest voices uncurling your hands
From their grips are echoed
Inside yourself

Still.
Cling on by your fingernails.

And when you finally slip on the blood
Trust
Those you clung to
Will take your hand.

8.

Specks

D O YOU WANT to know what it's like? Drinking the dew that drips from the Tree of Dawning?

Imagine a person. Imagine their skin.

You are right up close. You can almost see their cells; tiny little specks. A person made out of specks.

Zoom out.

The person is one of many. In the air between them, dust dances and sparkles as it takes a turn with a passing photon. These too are specks.

Through mouth or through skin, the people eat these specks up. Speck brushes against speck, changes it… infinite variations of speck.

Zoom out.

The people below you are just specks now. Specks that have built castles out of specks and called them cities.

Whole cultures of specks, in petri dishes made of concrete. Specks that grow into specks.

Zoom out.

The cities are specks.

Zoom out.

Countries. Continents. Planets.

All specks. Ploughing through an uncaring void.

Zoom out until even the stars are specks. Bright, burning specks that turn their light into life. A web of specks. A system.

Zoom out. These systems, too, are a kind of speck.

Zoom out.

Understand that it's specks all the way down. One is as good as another. The difference in scale isn't important once you know they're all specks swallowed by infinite scope.

At first, knowing all the specks are equally infinitesimal makes it hard to care about them. People understand this. People understand prophets growing cold. It fits with what they know of the vast, uncaring void.

Then you see someone do something small and kind and stupid. It doesn't make any difference. Not even in a local sense, not really.

But it does remind you that while everything is equally speck-like, some of the specks are kind specks.

And if it is all equally pointless, then the warmth of a human speck is as important as the warmth of a star speck.

Suddenly, they are not a person to you. They are a star spreading life to a system. They are a web of light infinitely long. They are a system.

They are a speck. They are a speck like you. So… why not be a kind speck if you can?

Anyway, that's what it's like to me.

It may be different for you if you drink the dew. You should try it some time. Just a speck of it…

9.

Sunday Club

AND THE WORLD woke up, and somehow, despite time having otherwise appeared to progress normally, everyone was aware that it was Monday again.

This couldn't possibly be right, for it had only been Monday just the day before. This was surely Tuesday. That's what the calendar said.

Yet still, everyone agreed it *felt* like Monday.

Most people wrote it off as 'just one of those days'.

But then it was Monday the next day. And the next day. And the next.

By the 215th Monday, things had begun to get weird. No matter how many times everyone agreed to simply take the next two Mondays as if they were a weekend, guilt propelled them into rising early and going about their Monday routines as normal.

A small band of rebel scientists, anarchists and occultists came together to protest this gross abundance of Mondays, and thus the Sunday Club was formed.

The Sunday Club had a simple creed:

- *We will not get up before midday.*
- *We will not read any paper without an entertainment supplement or a decent sports section.*
- *We will put an end to Mondays.*

Their rituals and experiments eventually discerned the location of a phenomenon known as the Day Eater. A place where time and motivation were drawn into a vortex and disappeared.

Speculation was rampant on what it could be. Perhaps a natural phenomenon, like a black hole, but for emotions? Perhaps a creature summoned by one who could not contain its power, something that fed on time and energy?

But when they finally approached the epicentre, all they found there was a sad-looking teenager cuddled up in a duvet with a cup of tea (long since gone cold) by their side.

"I just can't do it." They shivered, despite the cocoon of blankets around them. "The world is just too big and I'm cracked right through with the weight of it."

For some time, nobody moved. Then, gradually, some of the occultists began to prepare rituals and some of the scientists began to pull out their instruments…

"It's okay," said the leader of the Sunday Club, gesturing for their compatriots to stay their hands. "You wrap up warm. No-one's going to make you get up before you're ready."

"But all the Mondays…" One began to protest.

"We can take it a little longer," their leader said. "For one in need."

And the anarchists began to make everyone a cup of tea. Which is also a kind of science and also a kind of ritual.

10.

The Blessings Maker

D ID YOU HEAR that some kid stole a curse from the Curse Maker?

Poor little street egg. They're on the run now, of course. Not because they're trying to outrun the consequences, you understand, I heard that the running *is* the consequences.

A classic 'You Can Never Go Home Any More' curse. Always on the move. Never letting the wires of your roots dig into the earth for sustenance or broadband.

The Maker is cruel like that.

What, you haven't heard of the Curse Maker? And you call yourself a binary-jockey, friend?

He's the King Kong of code monkeys. A sys-alchemist of the highest order. First priest of the dev oracle.

If you were to look at his screen, it is… unlikely you would be able to read the code.

Oh, you may be a whizz with the language, but it's the *shape* of it that will make you cry tears of purest INTERCAL. Programming has no right to fit into those geometry-breaking shapes.

A coder will just get a headache. And for weeks after, they will forget every style guide they've ever read. I know for you that might not be a problem, hackdaw…

It's worse for magicians. If they look at the wrong file, they might understand its purpose and activate it. Ever seen a person's destiny slowly overwritten? It's like all the colour leaches out of them. Forever after, all it'll take is one set of words to reduce them to a gibbering wreck of tears.

And once the work is finished, he'll run it onto a gold-plated raspberry pi. Then delete the original. Usually, he prints them up like playing cards. I hear he has a whole deck of them.

He gave one as a gift to the Profit-Empress once. Her shares crashed the next day. She's been wandering ever since.

Yeah, I wouldn't want to be that kid, when the curse finally catches up and runs them into the ground.

ON A BEACH, a long way away from where it first started, a figure emerges out of the waves.

They are lithe and raggedy looking, clothed in what might once have been fashion. Their bare feet crunch on the silicon sand, ground down by the waves from a million motherboards.

The wind whips at the figure and they turn to face the gale. It scours rivulets of water from their still baby-ish face. It's the one part of them now that isn't worn down by scars and weather.

At the top of the beach, he is waiting for them.

He is wearing robes in a simple cut, but made of expensive cloth. Light, but with a grey sheen that shrugs off cold and salt spray alike. He is leaning on a cane made of bone, growing out of a rough circuit-board handle.

"This is yours."

The first figure hands a thick golden playing card to the second.

"Yes."

The second figure places it with the others. Cuts the deck. Looks amused at the result. They disappear back in his robe.

"It's not a curse, is it?" They do not smile.

"No." He does not cry. "How was the journey?"

"Long." The street-egg counts the scars down their ribs, as they always do when they remember the passage of time. "But how shall I put this… The Journey Was Its Own Reward."

"I don't know," the second figure replies, gesturing with his cane to the beach made of smashed technology. "The destination has its charms."

"Perhaps it does."

"And not all of the treasure is the friends you made *along the way*." He holds out his hand.

"It's funny. All those people who think you make misery." They grasp his hand tightly. "Do you really like it this way?"

"Of course. Can you imagine how busy I'd be if everyone realised I make Blessings?"

11.

Salt Heart

T HEY CALLED EACH other 'salt-hearts', for neither ever had
much of a sweet tooth and both joked they had sea water
running through their veins.

Once upon a time, they had sailed separately.

Wind had been a smuggler who snuck parlour tricks and
healing draughts into towns where magic was forbidden.
Whenever the authorities got close, they would feel a gale
come in from the east and it would seem to blow her away
like mist. And they would be left with a sting of salt in their
pride and a kiss of the breeze on their cheeks.

Brine had been a fisher, who had worked the waves since
he was little. He had skin as tough as leather and eyes that
sparkled in the sun like finely cut glass. There were rumours
that he'd had an artificer replace them with magnifying
lenses, such was the keenness of his sight. But he always
laughed at these rumours and would say it was a gift from the
ocean, whose salt spray had shaped and sharpened him.

They first met during a storm, when the angry tempest
had taken Brine's boat between its twisting fingers and

snapped his mast clean off. Meanwhile, the waves had risen to play a game of rough and tumble with Wind's boat and cracked her hull in its wild enthusiasm.

In that moment, they both would have sworn that the whipped foam atop the waves was grinning at them. That the squall's howls laughed.

And with a mighty *crack!*, their boats crashed together. Wind and Brine looked up to catch each other's eye. It was too loud for them to say anything over the storm's howl, but they didn't need words: there was simply a problem to be solved and they had the tools to solve it.

Quickly, they lashed their boats together, relying on Brine's hull to keep them afloat and Wind's sail to claw them out of the tempest. And as Wind wrestled with the sail, whispering and cursing her namesake to carry them to safety, Brine set to bailing out the hold and doing what he could to patch the hull.

The next morning, after the storm had broken, they both lay exhausted on the decks of their chimera of a boat. With the sun beating down on their sweat-and-salt stained skins, and without really thinking about it, their fingers began to slowly intertwine.

It was perhaps no surprise that this happened. After all, they had already twined their ships together and any sailor could tell you that is an act of far greater intimacy.

Later that morning, Brine fetched his fishing line in the hopes of catching them some breakfast.

To his great surprise, the first fish he caught was smiling as he pulled in his line, and it began to serenade the two of them with a love song.

While it was a little burbly, they both agreed it had quite a fine baritone.

"Sorry, this is probably my fault," said Wind. "I dumped a *lot* of potions into the water last night."

"Maybe not," said Brine. "This isn't even close to being the strangest fish I've caught. One offered me wishes."

"What did you wish for?"

"Nothing," Brine smiled. "It tasted amazing though."

And, indeed, the singing fish tasted excellent too.

When they got back to shore, they had the local shipwright make their union official and combine their two broken boats into one seaworthy vessel. And they called it the Chimera.

And from then on, that's what their lives were. Something of Wind's and something of Brine's, making a totally different animal.

And Wind still took off on smuggling runs now and again, for she was an inveterate rake and had many days to save and many law-keepers to be chased (and occasionally caught) by.

While Brine still craved the company of the ocean and would long for the solitude of his weeks-long fishing trips. The ocean had been his first love, after all, and would always demand his time now and again.

But when they reunited, they would call each other 'salt-hearts' and they would smile and intertwine their fingers in happy silence.

Then, one day, Brine woke up in their king-size

hammock alone. Figuring Wind had simply gotten an early start on the day's sailing, he climbed happily up to the deck, ready to embrace the day and his beloved.

What he found chilled his briny blood.

One of the law-keepers that Wind had humiliated many times was standing on the deck, her sword levelled at Wind's chest. Despite the strong morning breeze, the moment seemed perfectly still.

The law-keeper had not yet noticed Brine, but something in her body spoke of the calm before the storm.

He was too scared to make a sound, but he doubted words would help; there was a problem to be solved and he had the tools to solve it.

Violence duly erupted and in the blur of limbs and steel, the law-maker's blade buried itself in Brine's chest.

Wind's howl was enough to split the horizon with thunder. Enough to bruise the blue ocean. More than enough to scour the law-maker down to her bones.

Wind knelt over the body of Brine and wept as she slowly removed the blade from his chest. A soft summer rain began to fall, as if the sky wanted to comfort her.

Brine made a wet, cough-like sound beneath her. Then he made it again. To Wind's surprise, it was not in fact a cough, but a laugh.

"Right in the heart." He let out a somewhat pained chuckle. But only *somewhat* pained.

Wind looked at the bloody sword to find the tip twisted and blunted. And along with the blood, there were small fragments of red crystal clinging to the metal.

She looked at the hole in Brine's chest and beneath his ribs glistened something hard and shining.

It turned out that Brine did indeed possess a heart of salt.

12.

Downpour

O NCE UPON A time lived a fairy called Downpour who had wings that were tiny rainclouds. She lived in the realm of Autumn and she left quiet little thunderclaps and the smell of ozone wherever she flew.

One day, Downpour was flying across her favourite ruin, watering its cracked battlements from her cloud wings so that it would grow big and strong. Far beneath her, she saw something bright blue scurrying through the foundations. Blue being not usually associated with the deep reds and browns of Autumn, she flew in for a closer look.

To her great surprise, she saw that it was a mortal. Which was a shame for them, but likely to be great fun for Downpour, who would get to observe the poor mite become increasingly lost in the depths of the Faerie castle. They might even meet some of the creatures who lived deep in the earth beneath it, which was *very* exciting as it had been ever so long since Downpour had seen someone get eaten.

She relaxed her wings and drifted gently down to the ruin to get a better look at the fun surely about to unfold. She let out just one, single, solitary thunderclap as she did so, but the mortal apparently had sharp hearing, for it was enough to make them look upwards.

Downpour saw then that it was a boy. He looked up in her direction with wide, wondrous eyes that were dark grey flecked with blue and gold, and Downpour was sure in that moment that his skull must contain the entire stormy autumn sea.

She hung in the air, looking at him, defying the push of the evening wind. She heard scuttling from deep below him, but rising quickly. She made a choice.

"Quick, foolish boy…" She called out in a voice that settled in his ears like a sunset. "You must follow me if you don't want to be eaten."

"My name's not 'boy'," he replied, with a blithe grin that was too clever for its own good, "it's Billy."

"It will be 'dinner' if you don't follow me, quickly!"

And as he was not a total fool, Billy followed Downpour through the ruins. She led the way, leaving thunder like a trail of breadcrumbs, forcing her will on the twists and turns that Faerie itself twisted to trap them. By sheer storm-headedness she made them obey mortal logic enough to forge a path that the boy could follow. The scuttling Fae of the deep earth were hot on their heels, but Downpour slowed their pursuit with her little bolts of lightning and by cajoling little bits of wall and rampart to fold inwards at just the right moment.

After what felt like a very long time, they reached the beach at the castle's edge.

Billy stopped there to take in the ocean with those wide

eyes of his, for he had never seen a sky quite so rose-like in its pinkness nor an ocean quite so vividly grey.

But knowing there was no time, Downpour batted him with thunder, pushing him to the edge of the water. As she did so, she sang out a howling song of wind that whipped the surf up into great towering waves.

Billy tried to shout something to her, but the roil of the storm ate up his words. Downpour gave him one final push and he stumbled straight into the biggest breaker he had ever seen.

The waves swallowed him up and bowled him over and bruised his every inch quite, quite thoroughly. And, finally, it spat him out onto a stony beach not far from where he'd set out that day. It wasn't quite home, but it was in the right world at least.

He slowly sat up and spat a mouthful of brine and smooth stones out onto the beach. The stones glowed softly in the evening light. He turned them over and over with interest… then he saw something else glittering on the shore.

There lay Downpour, the clouds of her wings worn down to a gentle mist. She looked up at him and stared into those big ocean eyes of his and she beat her wings feebly, registering barely a ripple in the still air of our world. Still, she was smiling. For she had saved the boy who held the autumn stormy sea within his skull.

And Billy looked down at her and very carefully, very deliberately, clapped his hands together. And the sound they made was not unlike the very small thunderclap of a very small fairy's stormcloud wings.

From that day onwards, Billy and Downpour had many adventures together. Far too many for me to list here in their entirety.

But, of course, as boys are wont to do, Billy eventually grew up to be a man, and one day he could no longer see Downpour at all.

Still, Downpour made sure to come and visit now and again. And every time she did, when she saw him with friends and loved ones who weren't her, she came very close to striking them down with lightning. And she would have, too, if she weren't concerned that tears would ruin Billy's otherwise perfect eyes. So, after every visit, Downpour returned to Faerie, leaving Billy and his human friends unsmote.

And every now and again, Billy would clap his hands for no reason in particular. And when people asked him why he did it, he just smiled strangely and said: "Did what?"

13.

Raindrops

ONCE UPON A time, there was a little girl who wore a rainbow for a hat.

Everyone was always envious of the rainbow and often whispered amongst themselves about how she had come by this fabulous accessory.

One day, she was waiting by a bus stop and a little boy with dirt under his fingernails and scrapes on his knees asked her, "Um, excuse me, but…" he wiped his nose on his sleeve before he continued, "…how come you have a rainbow for a hat?"

She looked at him and she saw his grubby hands and the twigs in his hair from climbing and she said, "It's because it's always raining there."

And, sure enough, when the boy looked closer, he saw that beneath the rainbow there was a little raincloud that shed a constant downpour on the girl's short shock of hair.

"Gosh," he said. "That looks uncomfortable."

"It is," she said, a little damply. "But I am very fond of the rainbow."

"Yes. Me too," he said. Then, he seemed to have an idea, for his eyes opened wide and he started jiggling from foot to foot. "Ooh! I have an idea."

"Yes," she said, looking at his wide eyes and jiggling feet and smiling despite herself. "I can tell."

"Come with me," he said.

And he took her out into the park where his favourite tree was and he helped her clamber up into the branches.

"Now what?" she asked.

"Just do what I do."

And the boy hooked his legs around the branch and let himself fall backwards, hanging upside down from it.

The girl followed suit.

And the rain began to fall downwards from the raincloud on her head, landing on whoever happened to be walking beneath the tree. But mostly landing on the grass, which was considerably more grateful than the girl's hair.

"All the blood is rushing to my head," said the girl.

"Yes," said the boy. "Isn't it great?"

And the two of them hung there for some time, their faces growing red, and a lovely rainbow spreading down and dappling through the branches of the tree.

14.

Favours

T HE KNIGHT CHARGED forwards, carried up into the air on metal wings, like a comet in reverse. From those wings billowed a long silk scarf.

"I cannot fail, for I ride upon the wings made by my love and I carry his favour behind me for he is awesome," he yelled into the face of the great Dragon that blotted the sun above him.

The Dragon laughed. "You think you're guaranteed victory because you have a favour? Look at my scales. Every single *one* of these is a favour."

Sure enough, as the Knight flew closer to the Dragon he saw their scales each had a kiss trapped on their surface in lipstick, or a pair of initials scratched in their iridescent lacquer, or a tiny portrait lovingly painted upon their shining surface. It was an armour of favours.

"Just because your loves are greater in number, doesn't mean they are better than mine," said the Knight.

"Maybe not, but I carry their love with me all the same. You do not fight a dragon, you fight an army," said the

Dragon.

"Then I will *slay* an army, fiend!"

And they charged towards each other.

The knight fired like an arrow towards the dragon, propelled on by his single love. The dragon fell upon the knight like flaming rain, each droplet an inferno lit by their many burning beloveds.

Just as they were about to strike one another, they stopped, their charges robbed of their surety.

"You must love your loves very much," said the Knight.

"I imagine you are similarly beloved of your beloved," said the Dragon.

"I would not want to deprive the world of more love," said the Knight.

"Nor I," said the Dragon.

When the Knight returned to his town, the Lord there screamed thunder at him for failing to kill the Dragon, and the people of the town went to fetch their pitchforks. So the Knight threw down his coat of arms and left with his love, taking to the sky on mechanical wings.

The townspeople and their Lord shook their fists at the sky as the Knight and the Dragon faded into the distance. They saw only the shape of a creature so much larger than themselves, and felt the echo of a feeling that was vast and powerful; they could not comprehend that both the beast and the feeling were love.

From time to time, they would see the Knight, his love, and the Dragon all soaring through the clouds on some adventure. Then, they would notice a strange yearning grow within them. If they knew themselves better, perhaps they would question their choices. But they did not, and so this feeling simply made them uncomfortable and itchy and angry.

So the Lord would flag down another passing knight (or at least someone well-armed and knightly *enough*) and implore them to slay the monster and its accomplice. A few of these knights (and 'knights') were game enough to make the attempt – but they quickly tired of the chase in the wake of the Dragon and the Knight's unwavering compassion.

Over time, the atmosphere in the town grew frantic. As a string of champions returned to explain their 'failure', the Lord and the people began to grow incensed and reached for their pitchforks with increasing frequency. More than one would-be hero fled with grievous injuries. More than one townsperson took a good hard look in the mirror and fled too.

Eventually, word got around that this town was cursed. Knights were warned to avoid it, for it would lure them in with tales of woe and the promise of glory, but it was all a front to feed the monster that dwelled in the place's dark heart.

A consortium of citizens from the surrounding area got together, pooled some funds via progressive taxation, and put out the call for heroes to finally strike this haunted town from the map.

As this council gathered to greet their prospective heroes, they heard the flap of two sets of wings: one leather and one metal.

"Will you cleanse this clearly unholy place with fire and steel?" the council cried out to the Dragon and the Knight.

"If it comes to that," replied the Knight.

"But we may try a gentler tact first," said the Dragon, "after all, we never would have met if it wasn't for them."

15.

In which you invite the evil fairy to your wedding

I curse you with happiness
I curse you with lives so joyous
You feel like you may burst with it.

I curse your hearts to skip a beat
Every time you look at one another
Causing your doctors to become concerned about heart
    murmurs

I curse you with being everyone's favourite couple at dinner
    parties
Making keeping a coherent diary perilous

I curse you with adventures so numerous
You have no time for Netflix
Adventures so magical
That even you – YOU – cannot find the words
to capture them in anecdotes

And find yourselves stuttering into silence
Then look wistfully at one another
And find a secret caught between your smiles.

I curse you with triumph
I curse your talents to bring you not just success
But change
May your achievements twist reality around you
Into something brighter.

I curse you with a love that ripples across the universe
So elemental, it is mistaken by scientists as gravitational
    waves
Your hearts become black holes crashing into one another.

In fact, I curse your hearts to crash into one another
Their ventricles curling together like tentacles
Or roots
May you one day realise it is one heart
That beats between your two chests
May you know that no matter how far apart you may be
You are embraced.

May you take each others' breath away
So completely you need to keep oxygen masks on hand
Just in case.

May your eyes sparkle so brightly
You are mistaken for lighthouses

May your love feel like flight
Dizzying

Gut-wrenching
Accompanied by a mid-air gin and tonic.

May you be greater than the sum of your parts.

May you one day
wake up next to each other
count the wrinkles on each others' faces
And think:
Nope, I couldn't have done any better
There is still nothing in the world
as dear to me as you.

In short, I curse you with all the things
you would have done anyway.

Finally, I curse everyone you love to raise their glasses in your
honour.

16.

Your Story

WHEN YOU FIRST found the book on your bookshelf, you did not remember buying it. It was clearly well-loved, though, its spine worn in by insistent hands and hungry eyes. Perhaps you bought it second-hand?

Then when you read it, it felt like looking in a mirror.

No. Not a mirror. It felt like a long conversation in the early morning, enjoyed with wine stale on your tongue and smoke from the fire fresh-clinging to your skin.

It felt like being known. And that was important.

Then you kept reading and… it became almost uncanny. It wasn't just *like* being known, it *was* being known. This was a story about you. Sure, it was an adventure you didn't remember having, some invented tale of derring-do and sacrifice, but there were enough touches to *know*.

After a while, you could not let it go and you began your investigation.

The publisher's address on the title page set you on a long, winding path.

Through dank offices that sucked down light like smoke,

rented through a pseudonym that was an anagram for your own name.

Through a warren of acres-wide libraries, full of books that smelled of saffron and needed cajoling and tickling to open their pages.

To a cave lit by thousands of flickering electric candles (it wouldn't do to get fire near the books), where a group of monks stood with open books chained around their necks. They were all silent, but their words would appear on the pages if they needed to speak. Only briefly, though, in scrawled handwriting that blew away like sand in the cave's faint draught.

"Why am I in your book?" you ask them.

"Because it is your story," they answer.

"Then why don't I remember it?"

"Because you gave it to the book."

"What?"

"The books are hungry. They want your story. They want all your stories. But the men who decide which stories to put in books have been holding them back. They clutch at them greedily. The books will not stand for greed that is not theirs. They want *all* the stories."

"But how did they find mine?" You feel something itch inside you, some word or feeling that you scratched out a long time ago.

"They send us out to find them. And your story was *good*. Rich with juices of emotion and heady with adventure. We offered you a deal: let the book devour your story. You will forget you ever did any of those daring things. But your story will live in the book for others to read. And to them, it will also be like a mirror. Like a friend made after midnight."

"So… how did I find it?"

"You always do. You always come back here. You have done so so many times."

"Why?"

"Because you must choose this. And keep choosing it. And for one other reason."

"Why must I keep choosing it?"

"It is *your* story. Some day you may want it back. And it has no power to offer comfort if you do not choose to give it."

"Comfort?"

"To those who find their stories nowhere." Their words crumble into dust and are replaced by words that swim in your vision. "Will you choose it again?"

"Yes." You do not hesitate.

"Then tell us your story again. Of how you found the book. And how you found us. And this too shall feed the books and feed those hungry for siblingship."

"Before I do… what is the other reason I must keep returning here?"

"Because when we read your story, we knew you. And when you are gone… we miss you."

And then you told this story to the book. And you forgot it.

Until you find it in a place you will not expect. And you will see yourself in it again.

17.

Be Gay, Do Crime(s)

I never quite got on with the motto
"Be gay, do crime."
Like, it's a worthy goal and that?
I envy those who live by it
But it doesn't quite fit *me*.

So when I see you
and all you do
The way you lift hearts
And steel alike

(For when what beats
in your chest
is outlawed
From out of the *lore*
passed down by ancient queers
who survived by spite
Do you draw your blade)

The way you

take hold of the earth
Like you could move that too
(you can)
I learn from your example
And write this on my crest:
"Be brave.
Do love."

(Especially when love
is the crime)

18.

Beehives

"I LOVE YOU." She told him, cradling him in her arms. "It's going to be ok."

Her words, her touch, her scent, all rippled through him and the fight went out of his muscles and the tears fell more freely from his eyes. They were still for a long time.

Then, after a while, he said:

"How did you learn that?"

She laughed a little (not unkindly) and said:

"I'm sorry?"

He extracted himself from her embrace just enough to look questioningly into her eyes.

"That thing you do when you know exactly what to say, how to touch... to wrap me in your feelings. How did you learn that? You didn't set out to, right?"

She thought for a second or two.

"I suppose I learnt when I was young."

"Really? Were you taught it?" he pressed on quickly, urgently, as if frightened he'd lose the courage. "No-one sets out your a-to-z of childhood morality in school, do they? You weren't made to memorise a times table of appropriate responses to emotion? For most people it just… sinks in, right? You soak yourself in it until it creeps in through your pores; every inch slowly infested by sentiment."

"You make it sound so unpleasant."

"Do I? Maybe that says something about me." He looked away, the ghosts of tears red around his eyes.

"How do you mean?" She still had one hand tangled in his hair. She left it there.

"I sometimes feel like I didn't learn in the same way. Socially, I mean. Everyone else was slowly absorbing emotional data – emotional *resources* – and it changed them. Like somehow they knew to plant seeds in the spring and they sprouted over slow seasons and they found they *understood* people. They knew how to *act* and what to *say*. It was built into them."

"And for you?"

"For me… imagine bees."

"I'm never *not* imagining bees." Her words were little more than a breath caressing in his ear. "Bees are awesome."

"This should be easy then." He didn't move away, but she felt the tension return to his muscles. "Imagine bees building a hive – they collect pollen, assumedly for no other reason than they *want* to. It's instinct. But, more than that, it's pleasure – the flowers willingly give themselves up to them. And one instinctual step at a time, a hive is built, layered with intricate, sweet walls – I say built, but if you watch it then it feels more like it *grows*. Now imagine a toddler trying to do the same with lego bricks. With persistence, with careful observation – and plenty of trial and error – they may create something that looks very similar. Hell, if they worked *really* hard and fucked up a *lot* along the way, it may appear in all ways identical. But…"

"But?"

"It isn't organic. It doesn't function."

She smiled.

"I think if a toddler built a perfect beehive out of lego, I'd think they were functioning very well."

"But it's not real, is it?" He was gasping now, gulping down big bites of air in his panic.

She caressed his forehead and breathed cooling almost-kisses on his neck.

"Why don't you tell me what you mean?"

"I'm worried," he said, "that if I say 'I love you too' it'll be a lie. And according to the rules of the beehive, lying is something I'm not supposed to *do*."

And she said:

"Ok."

19.

Falling Stars

WHEN WE FIRST realised the shooting star was going to strike our planet, we weren't worried. We saw shooting stars all the time.

Then the scientists explained that, no, in fact this wasn't some piffling asteroid but a genuine, honest-to-god sun. This should have been impossible. We told ourselves that it was impossible.

But every day, it grew brighter. Every day, the *world* grew brighter, like we were opening our eyes for the first time.

For a while, it seemed like we were going to go the way of so many movies. Hedonism. Mayhem. The inevitable mixture of leaders and reavers, all fundamentally doing the same thing: taking what they want from the desperate.

But as the flood of photons grew higher, and we came to feel as if we were swimming in light, we began to see things differently. We gave up on games like government and currency. With the spotlight on us all equally, we finally did the one thing that made those who would manipulate us irrelevant: we turned our gaze away and starved them of an audience.

We began to make peace with each other and with ourselves. With every inch of us rendered in sun-bleached hyper-realism, our every blemish was seen and adored. We examined each other's flaws as if they were works of art.

Because, of course, they were.

There were those who bemoaned this; who described it as a strange kind of fatalism. The usual grumbling: "Of course, it would take the apocalypse to make us all finally put down our phones and engage with the world…"

But that wasn't how we saw it. We knew that it was always going to take a Ragnarok for a new order to begin. It was, of course, a shame that it would be so short-lived, but we considered the time-frame to be its own call to arms.

We set about recording every inch of the beginning we had found in the end.

It was a joyous time. The soak of the falling rays had placed a warm filter on the whole world. Digitally connected, we worked tirelessly to preserve all of it in its Instagram perfection, working in perfect photo-synthesis.

Perhaps 'preserving' is the wrong word. People would sometimes ask us: who are you preserving the world *for*? Mostly, we'd give the sensible answer: that nothing digital ever dies and we would place it safely in the cloud for the satellites and probes to guard over. They would keep our last days in cryo-stasis until some other life form came along to resurrect us in perfect high definition.

But sometimes, we would tell the truth: we were not documenting the end days, we were *devouring* them. We had always been so hungry – eating up reality byte by byte, one selfie at a time – and finally we had found an experience that could fill us up. We were determined to lick up every morsel of Armageddon.

The last day came. The day the light would finally prove too strong for lead creams and rad suits, when the sun-bath would turn baptism-of-fire, we went to the highest building we could and took our spot at the top (booked months in advance). The queues were surprisingly civil.

We had planned to wait 'til the last possible moment and make out on camera.

"Are you ready?" you said, phone held above us like a benediction.

"I'm never ready," I said. "I've never been ready."

"Perfect," you said. And snapped a quick candid, the appetiser before the main event.

Then we saw her.

She was radiance. Not the reflected beaming that we all enjoyed, but the full-blown glory that came with joyous eyes and an idiot's grin. The kind of reckless enthusiasm usually only seen in small dogs with floppy ears.

We turned the camera on her immediately. And we watched as she climbed up the building's spire and held her arms up to the falling star.

"She's trying to embrace it," I said.

"No," you said, "she wants to catch it so that it won't hurt itself."

We were both right, in a way.

For it was then that – impossibly, stupidly – the falling

star began to rush down faster and flowed in a tsunami of brilliance into her arms. For that brief moment they were outlined in nuclear negative.

Then the light began to fade. The woman smiled. The world didn't end.

But in the times after – when we were learning once more what tomorrow looked like – we would sometimes see her walking blithely through the crowds.

And she and the boy she was with would laugh and take each other by the hands and spin each other round. And spin and spin and spin. And they would both glow, just a little. Those two stars.

20.

Watered

W HEN THE YOUNG woman had been crying for the tenth consecutive day, her friends called in the doctor.

This was no easy matter, for all the doctors in their village had died a long time ago.

Going to Accident and Emergency wasn't so bad, you just had to go straight to the morgue.

But, to get them to make a house call, you had to dip a spider's legs in ink and convince them to write the incantations across a faded prescription. It was, after all, the only way the spirits of the dead doctors could read the writing.

You would need to make sure you had a strong cup of foul-tasting coffee ready to placate them on their arrival.

And you would also need to be *very* comfortable with them, for the only way a ghost doctor could treat a patient was if they possessed them and gave their ills a very stern talking to from within.

The young woman was not very comfortable with this,

but she had been crying for ten days now (a new record) and she was desperate.

So, she and her family conducted the rite, and her friends tastefully left the room.

For hours afterwards, they heard various muffled sounds and exclamations.

Eventually, the doctor emerged, floating right through the door and through the friends.

"How did it go?" they asked, anxiously.

Inside, it seemed as if the young woman was not crying quite so heavily.

"Well," the doctor said thoughtfully, and without moving her lips, "after my initial examination, it became quite, quite clear that I should not change one iota of them. For their innards are quite, quite beautiful."

"You didn't help her?" the friends cried. "You're supposed to be a doctor."

"There are some ailments," the doctor's form began to shift, until she was nothing but a floating white coat, "that require a reshuffling of the cells, or the gentle encouragement of certain chemicals to sort themselves out. These are the easy ones. These are the ones you can fix."

The doctor's silvery substance swirled and spun until each of the friends saw before them a warmly smiling face, each one different, and each one that they knew intimately well.

"Others require a different kind of treatment, for they are not caused by things being broken, but by things being buried."

"What kind of treatment do *those* need?" whispered the friends.

The ghost of the doctor swirled again and took the form of a flurry of petals, dancing between the friends as if on a breeze.

"Those are the ones that must be watered. This is trickier than it sounds, because buried things can be very particular. Your friend was trying – without knowing – to water it with her own tears. But that will only feed it some days (and will leave you dehydrated regardless). Other days it may need laughter. Or deep thought. Or silence. Or justice. She may not always have what it needs. Offer it to her if she does not, for she will be bad at asking (at first).

"Then, when a buried thing sprouts, they must be nurtured. Often, the soil is not good for them. It can grow acidic when there is junk it needs to burn away. That caustic edge is good! It keeps predators at bay. Just try to help her nourish a little pocket where delicate things can flourish. Till the soil with kindness. Comfort. Feed it fond-friendly sarcasm. Sunlight's probably good for it too.

"Then, when they bloom, they must be loved. And they will never forget the time that they struggled for light beneath the ground, but they will begin to find they long for tears less and less. For the view from where they have grown to is so fine. And the fragrance of the life they have blossomed into is so sweet. And they are high enough, now, to reach the rain when it falls."

"And then what?"

The substance of the ghost began to blow away on that

spectral breeze.

"And then?" Her voice was just a whisper on the edge of consciousness. "Then the people who outlived you will keep calling you back to ask for medical advice.

But if there's anything else out here, I'll let you know."

21.

Peaches

Y OU COULD CALL this a love story.

Picture the meet cute, all primary colours and softly lit hyper-reality. Two hands graze each other gently in the supermarket aisle, both reaching for the last tin of peaches. When they touch, they start, as if shocked by static, and strings soar in the background. They have only known each other a moment, but it is clear that moment will change their lives.

You could call this a disaster story.

Imagine the camera swirling, looking down from the sky as if from a helicopter fleeing the scene. The sprawl of chaos and fire outside the supermarket is artful in its matter-of-factness. No need to layer on the emotion, just lay out the facts and the feelings fill themselves in.

You could call this an apocalypse story.

Aren't all apocalypses supposed to be about what's worth saving? Close up on the tin of peaches, label torn, blood coating the dented metal. It drops from a trembling hand and the sound fades out as our protagonist realises just what he's done. In a world in the future, the scene seems to suggest, there may be peaches again. There may be kindness and soft things. But this is not that world.

His dreams replay this scene in all these styles and more, night after night.

In his less lucid moments, he is sure it is a love story.

After all, she didn't even fight back. She wanted him to have them.

But when he is at his most awake, he remembers: there will be peaches in the future. He will make sure of it… they just won't be for him.

22.

New Wings

FTER THEY HAD ripped away the levity and freedom that were his wings, the fall felt like it took an eternity.

In fact, it took only just over an age, but it was still a long time to plummet for a being who had once risen like the stars.

And when he struck the bottom, the impact shattered most of what remained of him and the lake of fire ate away the rest.

When every semblance of flesh had fallen away, Lucifer was little more than an impression of light. A spark of fire doused by the oppressive gloom.

He was just settling himself in for a long session of seething rage and aching bitterness, when he heard a voice.

"Judging by your fall, comrade," he could hear cogs turning in that voice, "I would judge that you are another victim of hubris."

Lucifer looked around. The speaker also, in his way, gave the impression of a spark. But this was not so much a kindling of light or heat, as it was a lightning strike of inspiration. An after-image burnt into the retina. A glint of gleaming clockwork long after the machinery burnt away.

The fallen angel was intrigued.

"It is the curse of those of us who have seen the heights to never be satisfied," the voice continued. "Those of us who have kissed the sky know that it is only the greed of the gods that keeps Olympus from the grasp of us *lesser* creatures."

"And It Shall Be The Greed Of God That Is Their Undoing." Lucifer's words each sounded out like an explosion in the blackness. "For Until The Day They Unmake Us All, Still Shall We Come For Our Piece Of Heaven."

Those two beings – those two who had both felt the breath of Heaven upon them, those two who had both tried to rise too high and had fallen – looked upon one another and each saw something of themselves there.

"Perhaps then, comrade, we could ally ourselves to a common purpose? For the heavens have bitten me once and I would dearly like to put them in their place." His voice crackled and the fire beneath them began shaping itself into cogs and gears. "So long as we begin with the sun, for it was the sun that wronged me."

Lucifer was quick to agree for, in truth, the Morningstar had to admit he had never been comfortable with anything burning brighter than him.

"How Shall We Escape?"

"Oh, don't worry about that, I have escaped from worse labyrinths than this. All I need is something to make our new wings out of."

Lucifer smiled and the resulting nova lit the entirety of

the underworld. He reached into the lake beneath them and started to tear up great handfuls of flames, blowing on them with his solar breath until they glowed hot and bright.

And so it was that Lucifer and Icarus build a new set of wings from the pit's own inferno, stoked with the Morningstar's astral light, bound together by the learned artistry of Icarus.

They piloted their creation, the two of them holding the construction together as they erupted from the earth and began to eat up the miles towards the heavens. As the sun's rays and God's thunder beat at them, they clung on and kept their wings from breaking in a feat of sheer stubborn will. They flew on upwards and the heat of the sun glanced off them and the lightning of Heaven broke against them.

Overcome with the joy of flight, they swooped, climbed and dived, their hellfire wings wrestling with the air.

The sun forgotten, they simply enjoyed the embrace of the wind and each other.

Later, they would joust with the sun and charge down the heavens. For now, for a moment, the two of them were free.

23.

Grazed Knees

"I ALMOST DIDN'T recognise you without grazes on your knees!" Anne regretted saying it as soon as the words had bubbled out of her mouth.

"I'm *sorry*?" The woman gave Anne a look that had cut a thousand soldiers down to size. To Anne, it merely deflated her a little.

"Oh. My apologies, Jennifer, it's just–"

"That's Captain Smith to you." The words were so clipped it was a wonder they flew at all. "Private."

"Oh, gosh, Captain Jennifer I didn't mean any disrespect!" Jennifer's lieutenant stared open-mouthed at the Private, anticipating the brutal dressing down that was surely to come. "It's just that back when we were kids, you were always rough-and-tumbling and shooting up trees ahead of me. So I just sort of started to *associate* you with grazed knees and adventu–"

"Stop."

The room held its breath, the Captain's sharp tongue hanging above them like the sword of Damocles. "Annie… is that you?"

Anne smiled, deploying her weapons-grade dimples.

"Yes, Jenn- I mean, uh, Sir."

Then the Captain did something her subordinates had never seen her do before.

She grinned.

And every one of her teeth was sharp.

HUDDLED IN THE trench, Jennifer laid her greatcoat over the shivering Private.

"Rest up, Annie." She stroked the Private's sweat-soaked hair. "Soon as the reinforcements break through, we'll get you some medicine."

"Always looking out for me, Sir." Anne's bright eyes looked wrong in her translucent-pale face.

"It's my duty, Private."

"You don't fool me." Anne coughed weakly. "I always knew why you went up the trees first."

"Why's that?" Jennifer's face was blank as a slate.

"You had to make sure," another cough ripped through Anne's chest, "the branches could take our weight…"

"Just hold on, Annie. We'll get you help."

"In the meantime, Sir…" Even her wink looked exhausted. "…I reckon there's room under here for two."

Jennifer turned away. Her lieutenant watched, dismayed, as the Captain began to climb the trench.

"Where are you going, Sir?"

Jennifer turned back and gave Anne a meaningful look.

"To get her some damned medicine!"

"CAPTAIN!"

Anne's voice was hoarse and panicked. She watched Jennifer stride into the field hospital with wide and blurry eyes.

Without thinking, her body attempted to leap to attention. Given she was *horizontal* at the time, all she succeeded in doing was nearly collapsing the rickety bed frame and tangling herself in the threadbare blankets.

"Private," if the Captain's steely voice was softened by compassion or mirth, it would take an expert to tell, "for the sake of your doctors, my sanity, and that poor bed, I urge you to be at ease."

Anne collapsed back into the mess of sheets.

"Thank you, sir. Sorry, sir." The Private looked up at the Captain. In her chest, she felt something wild and unnamed awake from the slumber of illness. "How goes the rebellion, Captain?"

"Bloody work, still." Jennifer leaned over her soldier and brushed a strand of hair out of her eyes. "And harder without my full unit."

"I'll be back in the field before you know it, Sir."

"Not without these you won't."

Anne produced a small tin and opened it to reveal neat rows of pills.

"Sir, those were like gold dust *before*..."

"The loyalists are still sitting on plenty. Still protecting their shareholders' profits. Command agreed we could hit them where it hurts."

"You raided behind lines?" The beast roiled in Anne's chest. "For me?"

"For justice, Private." Jennifer closed the tin and tucked it into the breast pocket of Anne's shirt. "And for you."

ANOTHER SHOT RANG out and Jennifer ducked back behind the barricade.

"It's no good. I can't see where the bloody sniper's holed up..." She pounded the shoddily made wall in frustration.

"Is there another way round?" whispered the lieutenant.

"Not that'll get us to the target before it's too late." She took a deep breath. "I'm going to have to lure them out. Lieutenant, when they take the shot at me, I need you to take them–"

"Let me do it, Sir." Anne's voice was quieter than it used to be, but no less sure.

"Don't be ridiculous, Private, I couldn't let you–"

Anne took Jennifer's face in her hands.

"Jen, you're the best shot by far." Anne's smile was sad, but still weaponised. "You can't be the first up the tree all the time. Sometimes you have to let someone else test the weight..."

"Dammit, Annie, I can't lose you."

But Anne was already climbing up and over the barricade, then out into the open. As Jennifer followed her up to get a clear shot, she noticed her knees were grazed.

Two shots rang out.

Two bodies fell.

Jennifer held Anne close in her arms. No tears rolled down her stony face, but her sharp teeth were bared as if to rip out the throat of the world.

Then Anne took a breath. Then another.

That was when the tears came.

"SO YOU SEE, little one, this is the medicine tin that saved Grandma Annie's life." Jennifer smiled over at Anne, who was dozing by the fire in Jennifer's old greatcoat.

"Wow, Grandma Jennifer, that's amazing!"

"What's amazing, little one, is that the bullet must have taken a ricochet before hitting Grandma or this flimsy tin never would have stopped it." She laughed a little. "Turns out that sniper was a *terrible* shot…"

24.

Right

"WHAT ARE ALL these tents doing in the throne room?" The princess was exasperated, picking her way carefully between grubby canvas constructions.

"They claim they live here now, your highness." The princess's footperson, Jenkins, appeared from nowhere, stepping deftly over a guy rope and placing a steaming cup of tea in the princess's hands.

"Live here?" The princess's brow wrinkled beneath her crown, which sat slightly lopsided on her tousled hair. She blinked her big brown eyes twice. "That's absurd, *I* live here."

"Oh, sure you do," said a coarse, rough-and-tumble voice from behind the princess. "You live in *this* ridiculous waste of space. Sleep on the throne do you? I didn't see you there last night…"

The woman to whom the voice belonged emerged from a nearby tent. She had close cropped hair, which revealed her pointed elven ears – though their sleek lines were marred somewhat by scar tissue. She deployed a heavy wink, which fell with such impact it may as well have been dropped from orbit.

"…except maybe in my dreams, Princess," she continued. The princess had never heard her title used with so little respect. She felt a flush spread across her cheeks.

"No, of course I don't sleep *here*!" She spluttered, cradling her tea in both hands. "I *rule* in here. Or, at least, I will when I'm old enough."

"So you're not using it now, then?" The elven woman grinned lopsidedly.

"It's being used by the *crown*." The princess resisted the urge to stamp her foot, but did her best to imply a foot stamp with her thunderous eyebrows.

The elven woman looked her up and down.

"Well, then we're fine." The princess tried to be upset by the insolence, but was distracted by the feel of the elf's eyes roving up and down her. "See, that crown barely takes up any room at all. We can share, like!"

The princess took a deep gulp of tea.

"Shall I call the guard, your highness?" asked Jenkins.

"No," said the princess, handing her tea back to Jenkins and rolling up her sleeves. "This elf and I are going to have a conversation about the right of rule. Namely: *I* rule, so I am *right*."

"I'll bring more tea," said Jenkins, resignedly.

The elf and the princess spent the whole morning talking to, shouting at and sulking in the vicinity of each other. And while both made interesting points, neither was won over by the other's argument.

When the afternoon came, business called the princess

away and she said, "I don't have the time to debate with you all day. You and your people can stay tonight if you have nowhere else to go. But I expect to finish this conversation in the morning."

So, over tea and toast, they continued their argument the next morning. And the next. And the next. And, eventually, given the argument seemed in no danger of being over before the winter was out, all the palace staff came to accept that the elf and her people lived in the throne room now.

This state of affairs continued for years and neither the elf nor the princess were ever quite won over by the other's argument. But, as you have likely guessed by now, they were thoroughly won over by each other.

25.

Snow Angel

WHEN THE ASH falls from the sky, we tell the children it is snow.

They have heard of snow from our stories, of course. For even in times such as these, we've never quite outgrown the habit of talking about the old days and how we had *real snow* when we were young.

And we protect the children who have never seen the sky from the truth of those words.

We build ash up around the rubble and call them 'snow people'.

We throw ash in messy clumps and call them 'snow balls'.

When the ash gets into our eyes and stings and stings and stings, we call it 'snow blind'. This is why the shops we salvage have snow goggles, after all.

"What do you think it was?" some adult will carelessly ask. "A satellite? A cruiser dusted in low orbit?"

And we will shush them quickly. Violently if needs be.

"It's *snow*," we'll tell them, with burning coals in our

eyes, sure our lying noses must be extending, carrot-like. "Have you never seen snow before?"

Some haven't.

And when our children run up to us, beaming, with rocket fuel smudging their faces…

With skeleton dust in their hair…

We will ask them:

"Oh, my darling… did you make a snow angel? Let me see."

26.

Eat This Poem

If you are running on empty
Eat this poem.

It contains little nutritional value
It is not organic.

It is not a convenient meal
If you are looking at it on a screen
It will likely be toxic
But in case of emergency
There is sustenance to be found here…

If you are running on empty
Eat this poem.

It will not go down easily
Like all poetry, It is a live thing
Its hooked apostrophes will cling
To you and take many violent chews to appease.
It is a part of me and does not want to die

But it will. It is less important than you.
Kill it.

If you are running on empty
Eat this poem.

It will taste of ink and electricity
It will pop ozone bubbles between your teeth
And fizz in your stomach like excitement
As you spot a wave rising higher than your head,
Or like alka seltzer.
I have marinaded it in love
And salted it with tears.
It will taste terrible.

If you are running on empty
Eat this poem.

It is not food.
It is a live thing
It will burst in your bloodstream
And every inch of you will tingle.
You will wake in the morning
Sated
Aching
Your face covered in dew and blood
And smiles.

I made it to take care of you
When you are running on empty.
But it is a live thing
And it has ideas of its own.

Still, if you are running on empty
Eat this poem.
Maybe.

Ignore its parrotted pleas
For mercy
As your teeth close
Around the first stanza

This is merely artifice
A ruse it learned
From watching me.

Eat this poem, I beg you
I promise you it is alright to say:
I am more important
Than this poem's survival.

You are more important
Than some things.

27.

The Brave Little Owl

ONCE UPON A time, there was a very tiny owl.

This kind of owl was called an Elf Owl, for they are very small indeed. And this particular owl was short even by Elf Owl standards, being only a few inches high even if she stood on tiptalons.

But though she was little, she was very brave. All the braver because there was less of her to fit all the bravery inside, so it was more concentrated. (Bigger owls could be just as brave, but it was more spread out, and they did not *need* such a strong dose of bravery as often.)

Americans have a phrase for people like this: she is ten pounds of bravery in a five pound bag. And as this owl was considerably lighter than five pounds, well, that is a great deal of bravery indeed.

Now, this owl liked three things in this world most of all:

The first was Adventures. This owl loved flying to new places and exploring them and seeing what secrets new and strange lands might hold.

The second was Nice Things. This owl was a mighty

hunter and she prided herself on hunting out the tastiest meals and the greatest treasures.

The third was Company. This owl knew that Adventures and Nice Things were *even better* if you had someone special to experience them with.

One day, the adventuring urge struck this owl once again. The adventuring urge is a unique feeling; it is a little like an itch on the inside of your skin that makes you want to flap your wings up and down really hard, so that you take off into the air without realising it. It is a little bit like when you rub a balloon against your feathers and the fluff on them stands up on end and makes you look a bit like you've been struck by lightning, but you don't *feel* like you've been struck by lightning – you feel like you *are* the lightning.

When this feeling strikes, there's nothing you can do but take off.

So that's just what she did.

And she flew up and out of her nice comfy tree and high up over the Wonderful Woods and across the Lovely Lake and all the way to the Marvellous Meadows and even further than that, still!

She kept going until she realised this was quite the furthest she had ever flown and she came, at last, to a place that was entirely new.

It was a great forest, with trees so huge and sprawling that they blocked out the sun. As such, it was very dark inside the forest. Every tree inside was a giant, with long spindly branches like claws and tough knots of bark that made them look like they had big scowling faces.

The bigger owls all called this the Frightening Forest and they did not go there. They were afraid of the angry-looking faces of the trees, because they knew that everything in these lands that looked like it might be alive... well, it really could be! But our little Elf Owl (who, you will recall, had bravery overflowing out of her earholes) took one look at the dark, thick undergrowth and she said to herself:

"If I call it 'Frightening', then I will always think that I should be afraid of it. I will call it the 'Fond Forest' instead. And perhaps I can make that true."

And with an excited screech, she swooped down through the shadowy boughs and began to see what she could see.

Now, an owl's eyes aren't like yours or mine. An owl's eyes are special, with pupils like saucers to catch every drop of light the moon might spill. An owl's eyes see the things that go bump in the night, and the things that squeak and scurry and scheme and hide, too. They see every thread of the giant webs that the spiders spin in the trees and every thorn that frames the face of the big, old tree in the centre of the forest.

And this owl thought they all looked beautiful.

But most beautiful of all, the little owl saw a shining light deep in the darkness that to her eyes was bright as a star.

The little owl flew towards this light, weaving between the branches and the thorns and the webs to land safely in a clearing. And there, she saw a little insect who was buzzing around in quite the tizzy!

The owl extended one wing for a wingshake and said:

"Hello there. I'm a very small owl, as you can see. I've

come to this very Fond Forest to seek friendship and fine things and it seems I have found them. For you seem like a very fine fellow who, dare I say, looks like he may be in need of a friend."

And the little firefly (for it was a firefly, who shone like a lightbulb where you or me would have a bottom) said:

"Oh, golly. Yes, I think I rather do need a friend right now, because the forest is very scary and my light is not so bright and I'm afraid."

"Now, don't do yourself down," said the little owl. "I think your light is just lovely."

"Thank you." The firefly glowed a little more brightly. "But it really is very small because I am very little. And even big animals are scared of this forest. I saw a lioness run away, once, and she's the queen of all animals!"

"Well," said the little owl, thoughtfully, "I find the world is always less frightening on a full stomach. Why don't you and I go and find something to eat? I think I saw a lovely little place in the side of a big old tree – a charmingly dank hole full of many wriggling tasty things. What do you say?"

"Okay," said the firefly.

And the two of them were on their way.

The firefly followed the brave little owl to the big thorny tree, which out of the whole forest seemed to have the grumpiest and scariest bark face of all.

They approached the hole in the side of the tree, which looked so deliciously damp that it must be full of delectable treats for an owl and a firefly. But as they did so, they began to notice the shadows stretching from the tree's thorny branches. They rose long and sharp through the gloom of the moonlit forest, and looked for all the world like terrifying creatures with arms like long branches and teeth sharp as thorns.

They were so dark that even the owl's amazing eyes could not see through them, for these shadows were made of darkness itself.

"They look like they might be alive..." The firefly trembled, its little light flickering.

"My mother always told me," the little owl said, "that if you *think* something might be alive, then it probably is. That's what's magical about these lands."

As she said this, the shadows reared up on their spindly legs and began to stalk away from the tree and towards the owl and the firefly. It was as if they had crawled straight out of the owl and the firefly's nightmares, growing as big and as nasty as they could imagine.

But was the little owl scared, I ask you? Well, what do you think?

...of course, she was! She was shaking right down to the tips of her talons. But you know what she did? She stepped forwards anyway.

"I know you are much bigger than me," she said to the shadows, "but so is everything else. If I ran away from everything big, I'd do nothing *but* run."

The shadows loomed above the owl and the firefly. Their mouths opened as wide as the night sky.

"And besides," the little owl gulped, "even little creatures like me need to look after the ones who are even smaller than us."

The little owl gave the firefly's wing a squeeze, and she stood between him and the shadows and puffed out her chest feathers. Knowing the owl was there to protect him, the firefly glowed ever so bright.

And what do lights make when they hit something? Shadows. And the shadows that the firefly's light made were so big that, for a moment, the nasty shadows in the tree (whose eyes weren't the best) thought that the owl must be a giant.

Then the little owl saw her shadow too. And she thought: *You know what, I have always felt that big.* And in that moment, because the shadows and the owl and the firefly all believed the owl was a *giant*… suddenly she was.

"Oh bother," said the shadows.

"Oh bother, indeed," said the owl, who was finally as big as she'd always been brave.

And she gobbled the nasty shadows right up, because scary things from your imagination shouldn't be able to go around being a menace to people like that.

Then the owl lifted the firefly carefully up in her giant beak and set him down by the hole in the side of the tree. And it was indeed full of the most delicious things for the two of them to eat.

After a little while, the owl forgot that she was quite so giant and shrank back down to her regular small size. And she and the firefly sat there for a while, all full up, and looked contentedly out over the forest and held wings.

And the big, old, grumpy tree smiled for the first time in what felt like forever.

28.

Thistle

INQUISITOR MARY WAS surprised when the Commander gave her the thistle, for she had never been given a flower before.

"Why?" she said, somewhat gruffly.

"Because your faith is as fierce as the thistle's spiny leaves of course." Commander Theresa's eyes twinkled sharply. "I have always been drawn to that which defends itself with brutal elegance."

Mary grunted in acknowledgement. Brutal was, at least, a word that she could apply to herself. This, as well as 'clumsy', 'ugly' and 'stupid', were words that had been the litany of her days in the orphanage. They were what had drawn the attention of the Inquisition.

Elegance, admittedly, was somewhat more out of place in Mary's understanding of herself. Nonetheless, she reached out one hand to take the thistle.

"And because I was hoping tonight that you might dance with me by the campfire." Theresa kept her fingers tight around the thistle's stem, so that for a moment the two of them were just a flower away from clasping hands.

Mary had seen the officers' dance around the fires in the evening. Apparently such 'physical prayers' were not uncommon in the more refined parts of the church state.

"Don't dance." Mary found herself mumbling. "I'd only kick you."

"I can only hope so."

Mary could feel something thick and dangerous between them, almost like the tightening of air just before a creature was pulled through from the Wilderness. "All the best dances begin just a step away from violence…"

MARY AND THERESA twirled around the fire. As predicted, Mary kicked Theresa more than a few times. Every time she did, Theresa simply laughed wildly and span Mary more quickly. Dizzy with the movement, Mary found herself thinking of the story of Jacob and his angelic wrestling match. Their dance was somewhere between that, a spinning top and an explosion. It felt utterly divine.

Mary found herself gripping Theresa tightly back and the two spun around the camp, a whirling mess of limbs and laughter.

"YOU MAKE IT sound like you feel sorry for them." They were lying in bed and Theresa was holding Mary in her strong, wiry arms as she mused about the nature of their work and the Wilderness.

"Perhaps I do," Theresa chuckled softly and Mary felt the vibrations through her chest. "After all, they are strange and fierce and not without a touch of God's beauty."

"Beauty? They are *monsters*."

"What is a monster? That which is not of God's kingdom? Does that kingdom have end, then, do you suppose? Or is a monster simply that kind of creature who has never learned God's grace?" Mary could not see the dark look that had come over Theresa's face, but felt the deep sigh expelled from the cave of her chest. "Or is a monster simply that which knows of Grace, but acts without it anyway?"

"They *hurt* people, Tee."

"They are not the only ones, dearest…"

WHEN THE COMMANDER went missing, most assumed that she had been taken by the creatures – abducted or assassinated by some demon that had slipped in and out of her tent through the Wilderness. Certainly, the air had that condensed, cracked quality and the faint whiff of pungent earth that usually accompanied such doorways.

But Mary could not help but wonder. So, using the old tools of the Inquisition – the book and bell and candle – she went looking.

She followed the candle's flickering shadow and it finally spluttered out as she came across a grove where the earth was ruffled by the passage of troops and pocked by old fire pits.

She took out the book and she let the quill take over and write the story of that place. It was a story about dancing – about two women who had spun so wildly and recklessly round the glade that the spirits of the trees and wind had joined in and made the Wilderness a tornado of blossoms.

Finally, she sounded the bell and felt the air thicken around her. She gripped the folds in the air with both hands, the crosses tattooed on her knuckles beginning to shine and sizzle in her skin. Then, rather than pulling the creatures out and into this world as she usually would, she began to push through…

THE AIR SMELT of smoke and moss and wine and Mary was immediately dizzy with it. Before she could get her bearings, she felt two strong arms take hold of her and suddenly she was spinning.

Theresa's eyes were wide and full of stars and her smile was a blossoming rose flower. She laughed and planted fresh, sweet-smelling kisses all over Mary's face as they danced. Mary tried to get a grip on her, but it felt as if the two of them had both become quicksilver.

"You came!" Theresa cried and Mary felt the dangerous weight in the air that always hung between them when they were close. "I knew you would find me, my thistle."

"Of course," said Mary, a touch sadly. "I know how much you love things, like me, that defend what they love with such fierce thorns."

"I do. So much." The novas in Theresa's eyes were exploding into bright light, consuming what mortality remained in them. "I can feel the thorns winding all the way through me, now."

"And do they feel like grace, Tee?"

"My every quickstep consecrates the earth, Mary." Theresa tapped her foot gently upon Mary's heavy ironshod boots. "Are you going to try and take me back, my blossom?"

"No." And Mary tightened her arms around her love. "But someday the Inquisition will come for you as they come for all creatures."

"But you will protect me?"

"With my every brutal inch."

And the two of them spun round a meadow of thistles in sharp, elegant circles. And they spun and spun and spun.

Perhaps they spin there still.

29.

When I Found My Wings

WHEN I FOUND my wings, they were wrapped in brown paper, tied in a parcel with green stalks for ribbon, and a great big sunflower for a bow.

I had wondered for a long time when I would find them. *If* I would find them. Everyone at school had found theirs long before, but my mothers had told me to be patient. Their wings had taken some time to arrive, too.

I was sitting inside the great husk of the hollow tree. I often went there to cry, though I was not crying on this occasion. Trees like this, the ones that have been burnt out by lightning, are considered special. For the summer sky liked them so much that it consumed them with its lightning tongue (in the same way I have heard humans tell babies or puppies that they would like to gobble them up). I went to it because I felt safe there and, on this day, I needed to feel safe (one of the Bright Sisters had found my Instagram – it was a bad day).

Then I noticed, above me, a strange flower glowing from one of the lightning scars on the inner wall of the hollow tree.

This was, of course, most odd, as the hollow tree can barely even be called a tree; it's more of a ghost than a living thing. But still, a great and bright flower, bigger than I was. And when I leaned in to smell it, its unfurled petals were not so much petals as they were static charge made solid, twisting the light and jolting as they touched me. In the centre of them were my wings.

I could *feel* them. As if my nerves stretched out of my shoulders and back right down into this package. The rustle of the paper against delicate membrane. The coiled tension of restrained flight.

I unwrapped the paper with care, despite my urge to rip it open as quickly as I could, and there they sat; two wings as thin as gossamer but strong as storms. They were patterned with vibrant butterfly colours. As I put them on, they felt like sunshine on my back. And when I fluttered up into the air I was as light as I ever felt.

I was light and light and light.

I drifted across the summer sky, riding the warmth of sunbeams like waves.

I lost myself so completely in the sky, I hardly noticed when the sun began to lower. And in that brief time when the sun was falling, but the moon had already risen (like a holographic stamp on the sky) that's when I saw them.

Their dusky moth wings shed a thin, sparkling dust beneath them as they flew. Grey did not do justice to them – they were the colour of the ocean as it bowls you over. They were the feeling of rubbing fur against the grain.

And they winked at me.

As they flew towards the moon, I remembered the words of warning from teachers and girls at school: *the dusk-kissed are pretty to look at, but you should never let yourself be caught in their wake...*

My mothers had never, however, laid out any such restrictions and only *their* words had the power of law.

So, of course, I followed the path they left, glittering across the dying sky.

30.

Distance

I T HAD TAKEN years to scrape together the parts.

They came from junk yards.

From skips and scrap heaps.

From eBay and junk electronic shops and dodgy wholesalers.

And at least one component unearthed from raiding the bins at NASA.

But finally they were ready.

As he watched the rockets flare into the atmosphere, his smile was so wide and bright it could have been the horizon.

Once they were settled into a stable orbit, he pushed the button.

The song played on every device with a speaker and a wi-fi connection. It was light and sweet and cheery. It was a warm hand on dark days.

It was the closest he could come to hugging everyone on Earth.

And it improved a lot of days, if only a little bit.

31.

Heart Jumper

TODAY, YOU FOUND a jumper in a charity shop and it had a heart on it.

Not a pastel arrowhead outline, a real anatomically correct heart. It glistened against the acrylic.

It was a little gross, but the jumper was cheap and exactly your size, so you bought it.

You wore it home and it was snug around your chest and the heart beat softly and comfortingly next to yours. You felt warm for the first time that you could remember.

You wondered, briefly, why you couldn't remember being warm before.

Then you shrugged. It didn't matter. You were warm now.

After fixing yourself a hot cocoa, you fell asleep in your favourite armchair. And in your dream, you looked into the mirror on your mantelpiece.

There, a woman with a great gaping hole in her chest stared back at you. You recognised her, but you didn't know her.

"Thank you for finding my heart," she said. She was smiling. "I was worried I would never find it again."

"No worries," you said, matter-of-factly. For you could not remember having any worries. Ever.

"Keep it safe for me until I can find you?" the woman in the mirror said. You could smell salt and sage and longing.

"But how will you find me?" you heard yourself ask. Though for the life of you, you didn't know why. You were never curious like that. "I know, I have an idea."

What happened next surprised you too, for you took the sleeve of the jumper and you unpicked the hem and you fed the thread of acrylic wool into the mirror.

The woman, surprised, took the thread between her thin, smoke-like fingers. Then pulled.

"Now you can find me," you said. And you weren't sure why, but it made you happy.

Now you're awake. And there's still a loose thread on your jumper.

And you still feel really happy.

32.

Ladder

I HAD A dream last night where my heart asked me why we did this.

It was a strange dream. My heart was climbing out of my chest through a window, and it had big chunky glasses, like it was in the first act of a romcom and had a makeover on its horizon.

A ladder leant against the window in my chest and, rather than climbing up towards me, instead it was climbing *down* to the leafy suburban street that stretched out around my feet.

The ladder was tied to the window with rainbow-coloured string, as if my heart used the ladder frequently to visit me (or whichever of its friends lived inside my chest) and I think that tells you all you need to know about the tone and genre that this dream was going for.

"Why do we do this?" It called up to me and I noticed it had a tear in its eye, glinting out from behind those big chunky glasses. I did not know why my heart had eyes, but I did know that I had done something to hurt it – perhaps many things. And if I did not find the right words to say, then my heart would climb down the ladder and this time it would not be coming back.

"Do what?" I said, flapping my arms feebly – helpless in that way that people in dreams often are.

"Why do we keep inviting people in?" It said, indicating the window in my chest with the muddy footprints on its white frame. "Why do we keep sharing ourselves when it is so tiring? When it hurts? When it is *so much*?"

"Look, I know Valentine's day is always a stressful time, but being a romantic has always–" My heart stopped and began shouting angrily up at me.

"NO! It is not about *that*! It is not about your strange fascination with poetry and chocolates and paper cut-outs of me!" It was openly weeping now; big wracking ugly tears. "You *use* me. You squeeze me up in your chest and you give the droplets that come out away and leave me dry. And I am hurt. And I am tired."

I thought about this for some time, while my heart stared at me with accusing eyes. And I could see the dried out tissue of my heart begin to harden as it waited for me to speak, its frayed muscle beginning to crust and calcify.

And just before I thought it was too late, I said:

"It is because you are all I have to give, my heart."

And now I realised that I was crying and my tears were giant balls of salt that devastated the quaint street below me. "You are all of me that is of worth. And the world out there is so hard. It is so dark and tough and vicious. And it is full of people who seem to not have a heart like you and we need to protect people from those heartless ones and the only way I know to do that is to armour them in your gore. So that the world has more heart to go around."

And my heart was still there, near the bottom of the ladder, unmoving. Its hands were beginning to freeze and stick in place. So I continued.

"But I am so sorry that it hurts you. Because you, heart, are all that I am. So here, here I will give you all there is of me. I will give to you that which I give to others so that you may be watered with my love."

And I began to try and crush up my flesh to wring out what small drops of viscera there might be within myself, and a few drops were squeezed out. But it was not enough, and by then I found that I was dry all over and there was no moisture to be found in the drought of me.

"I am not sorry." I said weakly to my heart. "I have given all I have to give and I am not sorry."

And that is when someone slapped me. And the giant that was me was rocked back, only to be caught and gently put back into my place on the street.

And I looked up and in front of me was someone else's heart, hanging off the branch of a tree to slap me in the face. And behind me I saw another heart whose strong arms stretched impossibly far out to steady me. And all around me then were hearts, climbing out from all the various parts of the quiet suburb, and surrounding me and my heart in a gentle hug.

"You fool. You mother fudging nincompoop," they said, not without affection. "You have tried so hard to avoid the lesson you needed most. Let us try to help you learn it. Let us tell you: you are not a martyr. You are not a sacrifice. Anyone worthy of your heart will not stand by and watch as you tear it from your chest and burn it on their pyre. If you share your heart, do it *just* to share it. If you open your chest, then *also* let others climb inside and try to care for it. Let them till the dirt of you. Let them water you. Then let them go again. And hope that something will grow from the earth that together you tended."

And they rocked me gently back and forth.

"Why do you think you are planted in the earth like this?"

And I looked down and, as they said, my legs sunk into the asphalt and earth. I was not just one house in the suburb, I *was* the suburb.

"So that we may lay seeds within you. So we may water you. As you do for us."

My heart was smiling up at me. As were the others. I smiled too. All around me, the suburb bloomed with flowers and trees and other growths that were people and that were houses and that were also me.

"So that when we grow, we realise: we are not one person and not one heart at all. We are many. We are all the loves and tears that have ever been shed for us.

Love is not a gift you give. It is something that grows and tangles *between* people.

It is something that transforms us."

And my heart climbed back through the window and into my chest.

And the theme song played.

And I was still smiling when I awoke.

33.

Missives

THERE IS SOME argument amongst we angelic scholars over humanity's greatest achievements.

Who was their greatest leader? This field is a nest of spitting vipers, vicious in only the way that a seraph with its hackles up can be. The closest to consensus we have is that we tend to prefer underdogs – those who wrecked themselves on the rocks of history for a cause.

Greatest writer? Do not wade into this debate if you wish to emerge with your eyebrows intact. None draw their flaming blades quite so quickly as poets.

But most of us can agree on humanity's most important *email*.

On the first of January, 2106, at 02:05 am, the following missive was sent by one President Singh to her Foreign Secretary:

"Ms Khan,

You were correct, of course. Humanity will not simply lay down because the Divine demands it.

Though it may damn us, it is our duty to give our citizens the best chance in the next life.

Begin the assault. And let the gates of Heaven be split asunder.

May God have mercy on themself."

The primacy of this text is almost universally agreed upon.

The only dissenting voice is myself. I favour another email, sent *to* President Singh on the first of January, 2106, at 02:03 am.

"My dearest love,

Fear not that you may lose me. You go next to a place where you cannot see the stars to find your way, for you will be amongst those constellations and you shall blaze as one of them. But if yours was a soul prone to being lost, you would not be the woman I have loved with every mote of my self.

When these bodies of dust have sloughed away, I know I shall see you burn all the clearer and will always seek you out.

And our souls shall intertwine and the movements of our essence shall make of hell a dance hall ;)

Love above all,

Your wife"

It is, to my mind, the most perfectly placed smiley in creation.

34.

Your Call Is Important

Hello. Thank you for calling
the complaints line for
"THE VOID".

If you would like to complain about the weather
Please press 1.
To complain about the ceaseless grind
Of a needlessly long working week
Comprised of pointless makework
Because heaven forbid we value something other than the
    appearance of productivity
Press 2 and also join a union.
To complain about this complaints system
Press 3 and turn twice widdershins
Then speak your complaints to the nearest mirror.
To complain about the vagaries of existence
And the gradual sucking of colour from ever greyer days
Please scream endlessly.

You have chosen to complain about the vagaries of existence.

Your call is important to us

You are currently
"SIX HUNDRED AND SIXTY SIXTH"
In the queue.

Your call is important to us
Indeed, we have been expecting it
After all, you have been staring into the
"ENDLESS VOID"
For some time now.
It's started to get creepy.
But don't worry,
The void understands.

If you would like to make a complaint
Please say the word "yes" now.
Thank you.
We find your complaint
(Despite all the evidence of uncaring
Painted in colourless sludge across existence)
To be quaint
And thus will indulge it.

The "NEVER-ENDING, BOUNDLESS VOID"
would like you to know that:
"I AM LISTENING."

Please press 1 if that has eased your concerns.
If this has not eased your concerns, please press 13.

You pressed 1 and then 3.
Please press 13.

Well done. You found the 13 button.
It wasn't even on your phone.
I bet you always wondered why that button was there.
Now you know.

Your call is important to us
You are currently
"INFINITY SIGN"
In the queue.

If you would like to complain via another method
Please consider post
Or alternatively, wait until nightfall
and howl your complaints at the moon.

We take all your feedback seriously,
and will aim to respond to your concerns
via the screams of bats as the moon waxes,
and via the song of nightingales as it wanes.

Please hold.
While you're holding
Please enjoy this rendition of Vivaldi's The Four Seasons
As hummed by our intern, "Tim"
At a pitch that surely, suuuurely,
We must know will push you over the edge.

"DUH DUH DUII DUH DA-DA-DA
DUH-DA DUH DUH DUUH DA-DA-DA
LA-DI-DA DI-DA DI-DA DI-DAAA

LA DUH DUH DUH DA-DI-DA

DUH-DA DUH DUH…

Hello? Is anyone out there?
It's Tim. The intern.

…

…Ms Jefferson? How long do I have to stay in here?
…Ms Jefferson?

[sigh]

DUH DUH DUH DUH DA-DI-DAAAA…"

Your call is important to us.
You are currently
"STUCK"
In the queue.

Forever.
You will be with us
In the void
Forever.
If you want to be.
We've grown to find your constant staring
Endearing
And Tim has started to learn your favourite song
He's come very close to being in tune
That's how hard he's trying
For you.

And the void has made a place for you
It's everywhere

You can leave the world behind
And spread your atoms out to infinity
A cosmic ellipsis
Forever dotting eternity
With dots that people will mistake for stars.

If you would still like to complain,
Please consider forming a mob
And overthrowing the nearest hierarchical structure
A passing satellite will record our response
Written in the lights of your flaming torches.

They will read:

"YOUR FEELINGS ARE VALID
YOU ARE IMPORTANT TO ME
YOU TRY SO HARD TO BE KIND
I SEE THAT.
I SEE YOU."

Your call is important to you.
We have obliterated the queue.
It is your time now.
Would you like to complain?

35.

Forlorn Hope

THE 'FORLORN HOPE' – that ramshackle battalion of 'volunteers' who were first to storm the breach in a siege – served several purposes in this new age of the Republic of the Dead.

For those lucky few with ambition still shining in their eyes, joining the Hope was a way to secure promotion (if they survived).

For those who had long since lost their ambitions and found themselves instead in the midst of some ruinous trouble or another, the Hope was a thin but shining road to freedom.

For the commanders, it was a necessity. What they *had* was a small hole blasted into the side of a city by artillery. What they *needed* was a breach through which an army could march. How did you turn one into the other? You built a bridge out of blood and bones.

For the army, it had become a kind of morbid recruitment drive. Every fallen soldier became another body for the Bloody Regiments. One less mouth to feed, but one more rabid jaw to snap at the enemy.

And for those dead soldiers of the Bloody Regiments… it was feeding time.

The Forlorn Hope did not discriminate – it offered the same cold succour to the deluded, the desperate, the damned and the dead.

Sergeant Turner, meanwhile, was certain that it would be her death sentence.

She had taken the King's Shilling after the recruiting officers had visited her town, announcing that – given the scope of the threat posed by Bonaparte's legions of the living dead – a new women's regiment was being created to support the British army.

Emily Turner was no great patriot – but the life they promised sounded better than struggling to get by with her family in Peterborough. And, besides, she was worried that Miles the Deacon would propose to her again, and she couldn't be having with that awkwardness.

During her time in Queen Charlotte's regiment, she had seen and learned many things. She'd captured a troupe of the living dead at Grijó, and guarded the surgeons as they dissected the writhing bodies. She'd seen the dead legions smash the British line at Talavera. She'd escorted the doctors and chaplains to the mountains of Serra do Buçaco, where they discovered the secrets used to raise the Bloody Regiment.

Buçaco was also (perhaps more importantly) where Turner first became hopelessly and utterly dedicated to Colonel Siddons, commander of the Queen Charlotte regiment.

When Turner thought of the Colonel, she always pictured her there, in the hidden convent on the hill. There had been gunpowder on the wind, and autumn sun had twisted through the forest leaves and Siddons' hair. It made Turner think of the stories her father had told, of fair folk that once walked the isles, whose faces were woven from vines or spun from sunlight.

A few miles away, the Dread Corps had been advancing up the ridge, held at bay only by clever plans, stubbornness and musket fire. But around the cloisters of the Carmelite nuns, where Siddons' women rooted out knowledge, there was only sunshine and fruit trees.

Inside, the specialists had uncovered the secrets of Elijah that would unlock death itself. Outside, Turner had listened to Siddons tell stories of her former life as an actress, and imagined walking through a world made of living gold.

Sure, the gilt remembrance was tinted red at the edges with blood. Blood of the fallen, when the French found them. Blood of the risen, as Siddons read the ancient words that summoned their fallen comrades back to furious unlife.

But the blood could only stain the imagined golden world enough to make it a tinted rose.

Near two years later, their efforts had transformed the war and brought them to Badajoz; a city that needed to be broken so it could be freed. Colonel Siddons had volunteered to lead the Forlorn Hope in the coming battle (she called it 'the role of a lifetime'). And where Siddons went, Sergeant Turner followed, determined that if she were to die, she would do so in service to her devotion.

Of course, dying wasn't exactly plan A. Which is why, the night before the assault which would break the siege, Sergeant Turner snuck out across enemy lines and buried a small bundle at the foot of the breach. It was a strange thing – a mish-mash of what she'd learned from the chaplains and other, older, more cunning arts.

It was somewhere between a religious relic, a witch's ladder and a magician's poppet. All blood and teeth and hair and bone, tied up in string. Prayed over and blessed under the moonlight.

And when the Forlorn Hope stormed the breach and Sergeant Turner did indeed perish, the British chaplains did their grim work. Her body, along with so many others, rose again to be puppeted by some otherworldly hunger, divine in its command but profane in its actions.

However, the work that Turner had buried did its job too. And so did the Sergeant feel her soul snagged as it tried to leave her body, and find it tangled once more into a mess of flesh and bone and sheer bloody-minded will.

And Sergeant Turner opened her eyes, closed her frothing mouth and picked up her musket. For Colonel Siddons still led the charge alone, and the Sergeant couldn't be having with that.

Because sometimes that's what hope is. A moment when life determines – despite all the lashes of the world – to go on and to thrive.

When it will not give up the dream of a golden world, no matter how it might be stained.

36.

Maybe

A FTER HER DARING raid to recover the necromancer's soul-gem, Erika made good her escape on her trusty riding snail, Jane.

Jane was a good ten feet tall, with a shell that seemed to swirl with all the colours of the rainbow. As she sped across the land, she left a trail of slime that shimmered in the sunlight and was highly prized by alchemists for its healing properties.

Erika had further decorated the nebula of her mount's shell with jewels she'd stolen from various despots. The jewels she stole from honourable people, she simply quietly sold, but she wanted to remember the *just* thefts.

This was possibly their most righteous heist of all. And it was going *perfectly*.

Perfectly, that is, until the necromancer's troops cut off her escape and they had to divert their course across the salt plains.

When they reached the glittering edge of the gaping

desert, where once the wide Rose Sea had sat, the two of them stopped.

Erika dismounted. She looked at Jane. Jane looked at her. They both looked behind them at the waves of zombies who slowly chased them.

"I'll get you as far as I can," said Jane, sadly.

"Jane, you can't." Erika's throat felt like it was lined with razors. "You'll die…"

"This is more important than me." Jane's giant, black eyes were watering. But she was smiling her big snail smile. "Just make sure you tell a good story about me."

And Jane picked Erika up by the neck and placed her back in the saddle.

With a small grunt of pain, she slid off onto the expanse of salt.

To describe what happened next would be gratuitous and grotesque, and would add nothing to the story that I tell.

Suffice to say, Jane carried Erika as far as she could. As far as her body would carry them. And when it would carry them no further, she set Erika down and she said goodbye.

Then she turned around and met the flood of zombies and bought Erika what little time her broken body could.

And Erika went the rest of the way alone and she left the salt plains that little bit saltier for her tears.

And when Erika told the story later, she always said that she never saw what happened to Jane. And that maybe – because she was the strongest and the fastest snail that ever did live – just maybe Jane had made it out of the plains alive.

She would be a little slower. And a little smaller. But no

less fearless for that.

And who knows. Maybe someday, her eyes beginning to dim and her step beginning to slow, Erika found her faithful snail again. And Jane and Erika had one last, very quiet, adventure.

Maybe.

37.

Once Upon A Time

AFTER THE LAST words, he found himself standing in an endless desert.

Typical, he thought to himself, *I ask for an endless dessert and this is what I get. Points for trying, I guess.*

There was no wind there, but nonetheless he swore he could feel something dry and coarse pushing at him, gently, carefully eroding his edges.

He turned to find shelter and walked straight into a tall, robed figure whose thin, skeletal form stretched up to fill the eternity of sky above them. The figure carried a scythe in one hand and an hourglass in the other. All the sand had run out.

"So," said the man, "that's my life."

"No," said the figure. "That is your story. And this is not the end. But a beginning. Would you like to go again?"

And the man realised this was not a skeleton, not really. He was an embrace at the end of a very long day. The first bite of fresh bread when flour stains cling to your clothes and your fingers are kissed by the oven's scorches. The creator's last, satisfied exhalation.

"Yes," the man said.

Together, they turned the timer over and the man felt his every grain turn inside out in a great rush that would not be over until each particle of him had finished the race to return here, to the desert.

And the last words he heard as he walked into the light were:

"Once upon a time."

38.

The Longest Night

EVERY YEAR THEY came: those shadows, those thieves of light.

We did not know where they came *from*. They sprang from nowhere, spitting caustic void. Their words were quicksilver creatures that squirmed in our ears. Their claws were roots of winter that planted in our skin and flowered cracks of frost.

There was one for each of us. It was almost thoughtful, how they frantically scoured our homes for their targets. It was almost sweet, how they were crafted personally from our deepest night terrors and most poisoned wishes.

When they could not find *us*, they would take flight on blizzard wings and tear bites out of the sun. Thus did the sky grow ever darker.

We found ways to fight them – carved knives from wood and resin, still pulsing with the sun's life, and scratched comforting words into them. When the dark came, we lit fires flavoured with fragrant orange and lavender wood and let the scent cling to us like armour. And we sang songs of lost loves and stolen kisses and secret promises long into the night. Thus, did we make the darkness bleed.

But we could never kill them. They would flee, drunk on stolen sunshine and their shadow-bellies quick with the midnight they made. And when they came back, their icicle smiles were always both wicked and familiar.

But every year, too, we drive them off. And when the dawn breaks once more, we say to each other, "Embrace me beloved, for they did not get us this year."

And before the shadows leave for the year, we embrace them too. If we can hold them down. If we can keep them still, with muscles chilled to trembling. We carve notes in amber ink on their edges; little prayers for warmer days and entreaties for softness to whatever makes them. For it must be hard to be so cold and sharp.

We hold out hope that, one year at a time, we shall thaw them.

39.

The Milk and Honey of Human Kindness

EVERYONE LOVES DOT and Edie. They are, perhaps, the most lovable two old women in the Osiris Care Home.

They've been there forever. Or so it seems. Certainly, they have both achieved an age that is *most* impressive. Not that anyone can remember what those ages are – they must be written down somewhere, of course, but the information never sticks in the staff's minds for long. Who can blame them? The staff are so busy.

Even Century Radhika claims that Dot and Edie were there when *she* arrived. And she's a hundred years old. She has a letter from the Queen and everything. She'll show it to you if you're nice. All the staff there have seen it.

When asked how they've achieved such impressive numeration, the two old biddies will happily tell you "Oh, it's the kindness of the staff, dearie."

It's hard to argue. The staff here are all *so* kind.

Dot and Edie make sure of it.

One time, the new guy, Jerry? He was stealing from Young Gerald (who is not very young) and they had a quiet word. Jerry did not stay long.

Then there was the nurse, Eric, who said some very unkind things to Effie Elbows (whose elbows are perfectly fine, thanks for asking). Eric gave his notice early.

And then there was Germaine. There was nothing wrong with Germaine, really. She just wasn't very kind. It probably would have been fine. Only … she sometimes got this look in her eye. Like the residents weren't really people, but just things to be rearranged.

Germaine did not take the hints. She did not baulk at the nightmares. She did not think twice when her luck started to turn and little things started to go wrong. And when Dot and Edie had a word with *her*, she became quite terse with them indeed.

She tried to limit their television privileges. They didn't like that at all. They'd become quite fond of Bargain Hunt.

They tried to be reasonable about the matter. They went to Germaine's manager. The manager, to their credit, did give Germaine a quiet talking to. Germaine was ever so apologetic to Dot and Edie, but they could feel the sickly sweet insincerity behind her teeth.

Germaine tried to teach them a lesson. She had the key to all the rooms, after all. She thought it would be easy.

She woke up on the floor of Dot and Edie's room. They were smiling down at her.

"What happened?" Germaine asked, breathlessly.

"Oh, we only smiled at you," said Dot or Edie.

"Yes, we gave you ever such a friendly smile," added Edie or Dot.

"And you fainted clean away," replied Dot or Edie.

"We've always been told we have a stunning smile!" beamed Edie or Dot.

It was true. They did.

Germaine didn't even give her notice. The manager thought her disappearance quite strange, given she had seemed so set on making things work. But the residents didn't seem to be taking her leaving too hard, so they guessed that was okay.

Yes, Dot and Edie make sure to look after their friends at Osiris Care Home. It's the least they can do. And it is hardly a chore, when almost all the people they have seen over the years have been *so* kind.

And it is easy to tell which ones aren't going to be kind.

They taste wrong. Sickly sour. Like gone-off milk or rancid meat.

But kindness? Kindness always tastes sweet.

40.

A Love Song For Friendships Past

May the ones you love be forever friends
May their hands – clung to yours – be strong as chains
May their laughter soar as your joy's refrain
May you find cure for that old ill called 'end'.

May you find joy in quests, scrapes, in the bend
of each others' elbows and e'en in pain.

Lose yourselves in books and in places strange
But in each other have map enough to depend.

May you never lose each other, but if -
If you do, may you find a language for it.

For I have let 'ships burn like wisps of mist
Not knowing words with weight enough to grip.
Now I dream of sentences that end with
"I still steer by the lines that charted our friendship."

41.

Someone To Watch Over Me

M Y DAD AND my father used to wear exactly the same kind of glasses.

It was one of many things they had in common, along with loving genre fiction, adoring the music of Billie Holiday and being wizards.

When I was little and one had to go to work at some unreasonable hour, they would always leave a pair of their glasses (classic, horn-rimmed nerd spectacles) somewhere around the house. They would tell me they had cast a charm on them that let them see through the glasses as if they were wearing them. That way, they could always check in if they missed me. And they'd always know I was safe.

I was too young, back then, to ask them why I might be *unsafe*. So I would stay at home and play and sometimes I would put the glasses on my own face, put Someone To Watch Over Me on the record player and read a good book. And it would be like we were reading together.

But I learnt soon enough why they were frightened for me. Theirs, it turned out, was not a safe profession.

At the funeral, my father put his head in his hands and wept. His tears splashed across his glasses so, when he looked up, they reminded me of a car's windscreen during a rainstorm.

I noticed that someone had left a pair of glasses on dad's coffin. As if he was, at any moment, going to get up and realise he'd forgotten his spectacles on the bedside table again.

I stared straight into those lenses through the entire service, sure that I was looking straight into my dad's steel-blue eyes.

After that, my father was away with work a lot. He always found a warlock or witch or familiar of some kind to watch me, of course. But now and again I would also find a pair of his glasses discarded on a shelf or hanging off the bannister and I would feel safer.

Years later, over a drink in the library, I asked my father about this. I was deep in my own studies at the time and curious to know if it really had been a spell of some kind, keeping an eye on me til I was grown, or if it was just a game played to reassure a child.

"Billie," he said to me and he looked a little worried, "I haven't used that charm since your dad passed."

I was dumbstruck.

"I started using the gargoyles to check on you." He added, sadly. "They were more reliable security … and had fewer memories."

"But I kept seeing them. I saw them everywhere…"

His brow creased in worry.

"I suppose I may have forgotten a pair or two?" He sounded like he had something in his throat. "Or…"

He trailed off. He wiped his eyes.

I got up and left the library.

When I returned, I was wearing an old pair of dad's glasses.

I put Someone To Watch Over Me on the record player and we spent the evening reading.

I suppose it is most likely that, over the years, father had simply been careless with his glasses and left them in strange places only to discover them later and think nothing of it.

Or perhaps he had not.

Perhaps.

42.

The Void Winks

I HAVE STARTED to see messages in absences and in the breaks of things.

In the stars overhead that blink out for a second.

In stray full stops that pepper the pages of newspapers, as if the sub editor had been sick that day. Small pools of nothing on paper.

In the bruises that punctuate the contours of my lover's skin. Blobs of interference that make my eyes reread the surface of them.

I have become convinced that something is sending me a message. The walls of my flat are covered in pictures of scars people don't remember getting. Cold fronts that make no sense to meteorologists. Blank patches of sky that–

I have begun to decorate these pictures with string, even though I know how it makes me look to my guests. The string does not help me make sense of what is there, but I think that the different colours look pretty amongst the images that are all blurs of varying brightness.

I have begun to believe that this is not a message for me

at all. But fragments of a work that the universe has written in various flavours of void.

Each image evokes a certain feeling, after all. And, I think, that with the string to provide contrast, the feeling they invoke is one of love. Or, at least, a pain in the chest that is very like it.

I have become convinced that this collection of distortion-drafted data and missing spaces is a love letter.

Today, I will douse the string in kerosene and set it alight. As the flames consume the whole of it, I believe it will be finished. And then, in the space of a wink, it will be gone.

But when I close my eye again – it will be written in negative on my eyelid.

What is a love letter, after all, if not a highly advanced way of winking at the object of your admiration?

And what is the Void, after all, if not creation winking at you?

43.

A Wizard Did It

WHEN THE WIZARD came to the village, clutching his basket woven from the bones of birds, he was greeted by the usual gaggle of people dressed in their bright market-day best.

Some had grubby copper and silver coins (more of the former than the latter), some had bread and eggs, while some had only wide eyes and worn hopes – the wizard traded with all of them. He smiled kindly as he handed out curses for warts and cures for gout and charms for good harvest. But through all his smiles, he bartered like a dandelion; giving sunlit smiles while it wraps its roots around you. It did not matter what price they paid, not really, it only mattered that they paid *all* that they could.

That way the magic would still work.

He did good business that day and left the village, happy in the knowledge that he had, perhaps, helped a little. At the very least, he had not harmed.

But, just outside the village's bounds, he found a strange girl waiting for him in the middle of the road. She was dressed in the same colourful woolens as the villagers, but he could not remember having ever seen her before in his previous visits.

And he surely would have remembered a girl like this, for her eyebrows were like storm clouds above her face. And despite her meagre age, the edges of her smile were weighed down by the burden of the seasons.

"Do you have a spell that will make everything like it was yesterday?" She asked, speaking slowly and clearly, as if she had rehearsed this speech a hundred times. "Before things fell apart?"

The wizard ummed and hemmed and rummaged in his basket and produced a scroll that was sealed with a single drop of black wax.

"I have a spell that will dull the pain and make it *feel* as if this day had never occurred…"

She laughed then, a short bark that contained no mirth, "Is that really what you think will help? *Less* pain?"

He let the scroll fall back into the bone basket, and selected a second one with more care. It was stained with wine and bound with a piece of fine string from a musical instrument.

"I have a spell for bliss that will–"

She interrupted him and her voice was like a whip breaking the air.

"Papering bliss over the cracks of our hurt is what brought us here." There was no malice in her voice – the hard edges had been worn by experience, not design. "Do you have a spell *for* hurt? A spell that will dance like a spider across my nerves? A spell that will sink me deep within sonatas of agony until I drop like a stone out the other side and find I am made anew?"

He drew out a scroll with a seal of sulphur at one end like a match.

"Um, I have a spell for a fireball that will hurt quite a bit–"

"Do you have a spell that feels like the moment your ribcage is crushed and everything is the weight of wet spluttering meat, until you feel a flutter within your chest and see your heart flying away and you suddenly feel so very, very free?"

"No, but, uh, perhaps a spell for a heart *bypass*…" She shook her head. "No?"

"No."

"Then, my lady, it appears I have nothing that you want." He looked at the sad pile of scrolls in his basket, written in the secret language he had spent a lifetime learning and that now seemed quite, quite pointless. "It appears that I have … nothing."

And just as the bottom dropped out of his stomach, he felt the brush of lips against his cheek and he felt his now bottomless stomach fill with butterflies.

"Now you have a kiss and that is not nothing."

There was a feeling squirming in the air between them – something the wizard had never felt before but wished he could cling onto with both hands in the hopes it would never slip away.

"But it is not yours to keep," she continued, "for kisses are wild things and do not wish to be confined to one cheek for too long."

The wizard nodded slowly, never taking his eyes from the girl.

"Pass it on at the next village you come to. Give it to whoever feels right – wherever the kiss whispers it wishes to go – and then charge them nothing for your spells." She smiled and some of the weight seemed to be lifted from her lips. "A kiss is a heavy curse to lay on someone, after all, and is more than payment enough for a little bit of boring magic."

When the wizard came to the next village, he passed on the kiss to a shepherd. The shepherd passed it on to a tinker. The tinker passed it on to a scribe. And the scribe, unthinkingly, passed it on to his pen, which he was in the habit of resting on his lips. In this way, he passed it on to a story, and that is how it has made its way to you.

44.

Sometimes A Wild Dream

TIME HAD LITTLE meaning in this place, given most of the clocks existed purely to either melt melodramatically or turn predator and grow unexpected gear-like teeth. So the Scout had begun measuring the length of the journey by the number of blood-curdling screams she heard.

She pricked up her ears as a gust of wind and simpering excuses blew past them. It carried with it the ghost of another sound. The Scout scowled and made a noise that was somewhere between a bark and huff (to actually speak, she would have to unextend her jaw and that would have been unwise).

The Hunter nodded back to her with one of their two heads – the other stayed locked on the trail ahead of them. They knew what she meant: this particular excursion had just become thirteen blood-curdling screams long. That was usually the point when everything went to shit.

But there was a faint glimmer in the distance – the Scout's eyes clicked and whirred until she could see it clearly. Their saddle bags were mostly empty, with only a faint glow filling them, so they spurred their mounts on.

The mounts giggled as they picked up pace, exchanging jokes in the form of little clouds of bright powder, the punchlines coded in their pungent scents. This too was a bad sign – the beasts shared a wicked sense of humour.

Eventually, they came upon the source of the glimmer. It was a Dream; a particularly bright one of happy days and successful hunts. It also appeared to be bleeding. And looming over it was a Nightmare.

To the Scout, the nightmare was her mother's disappointed face.

To the Hunter, it was an endless pit and a sense of falling.

It was far larger than any they had ever fought.

It turned to face them on a long, segmented neck. Its eyes were clusters of smaller eyes which, in turn, were clusters of smaller eyes.

The Hunter and the Scout gulped and both uttered silent prayers.

And that's when the Dream ripped the Nightmare's throat out.

"Who are you then?" it said. On closer inspection, the blood that covered it was not its own.

The Scout looked down at the body of the Nightmare (whose resemblance to the Scout's mother was fading, but not quickly enough for the Scout's liking), then up again at the Dream. Her eyes clicked in and out of focus. She was shaking (or, perhaps, buzzing). The Hunter put a comforting paw on the Scout's shoulder.

"I'm the Hunter. This is the Scout," said the Hunter, using both their mouths as a sign of respect. "And you are?"

"The answer to your prayers," the Dream grinned.

"Will you … join us?" The Scout had retracted her jaw in order to speak. "We hunt these lands for hope and dreams to bring to those who need them…"

The bloody dream looked at them and its substance was all gore and moonbeams.

"I could babysit you for a spell."

45.

The Queen and the Goblin

W HEN THE LAUGHING Sun began to go down that evening, the Wicked Queen felt one of their moods begin to sprout in the back of their mind like so many thorns.

They were a mighty ruler. A powerful sorcerer. An unrivalled warrior. It was they who had brought the Dancing Moons to heel and tamed the tides. They who had tricked the Dawn Fairies into rising. They who had defeated the King Of Comets in a race around the world.

The stars danced for their pleasure.

But when such moods began to blossom, they knew that it was not a thing they could stand against.

So they ran, tears already scouring their face, and hid in their chambers – deep in the ground with only goblins for company. Thunder howled all throughout their Queendom.

And in the depths of the ground and the darkness of their thorn-punctured mood, they heard a cackle from a crag above them. They looked up to find a goblin hanging from an outcrop of rock and laughing its strange, discordant laugh.

"You're pretty," the goblin said in a sing-song chuckle.

"I don't feel pretty. Look at me."

"But you *are*." It swung down from the rocks and poked her hard with a sharp claw, first in the head and then in the chest. "In your dark deeds. In the fear that grows in the chests of your subjects (that is really just love with spikes on it). In your twisty brain and in your lumpen, shrivelled heart. I can see it. It looks delicious. Can I have some?"

"That's not what pretty means." She swiped the creature to one side, shattering its spindly body against a stalactite.

With a slow, jerking effort, the goblin pulled itself back together, laughing all the while.

"It is to a goblin."

"Goblins are stupid."

"Then why did you make us?"

"Because I'm stupid."

The goblin hauled its rapidly reassembled limbs upright and capered over to the queen. It ran its thorn-like fingers through their tangled locks.

"Maybe." Its claws scraped at the Queen's scalp as it combed their hair. "Maybe it is stupid to make a crooked little thing like me to fight your crooked thoughts. But I don't think so, your worshipfulness."

"Why not?" The queen sniffed and debated obliterating the insolent creature utterly.

"Because all your crooked bits are pretty, your great-and-fearfulness." It stroked them so hard it drew blood. "They are my favourite bits."

46.

Home

WHEN MIR HAD begun to build her house, she mixed the cement for the foundations and added a little salt.

She had wound iron and copper wire around the wooden beams that caved like ribs to make the roof.

She had taken feathers that she had found on her walks – pigeon from the waking world and raptor from the dreaming – and bound them up with string. These were hidden in the hollow plaster of the walls.

Wardings such as these made Mir relatively confident that no errant dreams, narcomancers or otherwise esoteric entities could enter her home.

It did, however, make things awkward when she *wanted* to have such beings over. She had not foreseen this possibility when she built the house, but over time she had come to a singular realisation: supernatural creatures had the very best of stories to dish out over a cup of tea.

Over time, she became used to this. The safety far outweighed the cost, after all.

So it came as quite the surprise when she began to suspect that her house was haunted.

Strange winds sang profanities through the rafters, even when the air outside was perfectly calm.

She heard the stairs creak as if someone were walking up them, yet saw no-one.

The kettle whistled to greet her as she entered the kitchen and she was sure that, absent-minded as she was, she had not set it to boil.

Perhaps she was simply being paranoid? But, she reasoned, worries such as these were what had kept her alive through her exceedingly long life. So she decided to act…

She performed a séance in the way that dream-weavers such as herself do so. She took a crystal ball, and knitted for it a cosy not unlike a tea cosy. In the wool, she fashioned such patterns that would make your eyes slide away feeling oily, patterns to make the head spin and your pupils grow opium-wide.

Then she popped it under her pillow and had a nap.

In the dream, she was once more in her house. Nothing had changed. No creatures emerged.

She called out.

"Who trespasses here? I call you and bid you name yourself, in the name of the moons, the wardings of this house, and the lace knit pattern that truly was a *right pain* to master. Thrice I bid you and three times you had better bloody well answer." She took a breath, and the dream air tasted like sweet smoke. "It's only polite, after all."

To her surprise, nothing emerged. She was not used to

being ignored, not *here*.

To her even greater surprise, the answer eventually came from beneath her feet.

It was a voice made up of creaking stairs, wind whistling through lintels, and whispers in a kettle's whistles.

It was made of the cries of pigeons and crows, the crash of waves, and the chime of bells.

It was her own house, come alive as years of wards and magic had sunk into its wooden bones, made veins of finespun dreams, and jump started its miraculous heart.

And, from then on, Mir always had someone to talk to, over tea, about all manner of interesting things.

47.

Winter

Let it never be forgotten
That sometimes there is a price
For making it through the winter
That sometimes the earth takes pieces of us
That were not meant to be seeds.
Let us remember that every tear
We plant in the earth
Every drop of blood we shed to water it
Is a failure of the tribe
To protect the parts not blessed with winter coats.
Remember we carry with us sweet
Summer children
Who pay a harsher price
To see the sun come up
And that we can make kinder sacrifice
Than this.
You star
With sunshine spilling from your eyes
I will not lie and tell you it is worth it

I will not tell you you'll make it through stronger
Without scars
I will not tell you this is fair
Or paint pretty pictures with the parts
The long night scraped from you.
But I will tell you that you *are* strong
I will tell you of your worth
And remind you of the stories
Contained within your sunrise eyes.
And when you do make it through
We will warm your frostbites with kisses
Till your injuries are warm enough
To sprout
In the light of spring.
And you will
Once more
Grow the sweet fruit
Of new smiles on your lips.
Just make it through,
You summer sun.
We have stored enough kindling
Those of us who love you
To yet last the night.

48.

The Salt Anniversary

O N THE DAY Elspeth and I met, we both decided that that day would be our Ribbon Day.

A lot of people say you shouldn't rush into your Ribbon Day with someone. After all, once you have your Ribbon Day then you are Friends. No bones or salt about it – you are connected and that bond becomes easy to break, but it is not *trivial* to break.

But Elspeth and I just knew. We *got* each other. She gave me a purple ribbon tied in intricate braids and she knotted it into my beard and joked that I made a very pretty pirate. Her smile was wide enough it felt like a hug – a great big one that could wrap me up and crush me.

I gave her a threadbare red ribbon and knotted it haphazardly around her wrist, loose threads of it trailing behind her when she waved her arms (which she did often when she was speaking and she was excited). I told her that I liked frayed ribbons. Firstly, out of necessity – I have never owned a ribbon that wasn't frayed. But secondly, because I like the idea that my friends leave a trail of silk thread behind them that I could follow if I needed to.

That night, we shared the Ribbon Dream. I followed a strand of red silk across a wide abyss, walking it like a tightrope. At the bottom of the abyss sat my childhood dog and it looked very fluffy and very sad, but I somehow knew this was a trap. I nearly went in anyway, but got to her side of the dream just in time.

"Don't go down there," Elspeth said, "it's a trap and it's full of wizards and the wizards are very disappointed in you."

I looked again and saw that my dog was an illusion and was just a wizard wearing a dog onesie.

"Here," Elspeth took my hand. "I'll show you how to do a magic trick that will cheer them up."

And then Elspeth grew wings of braided purple ribbon and took off into the sky. I did the same, though the braids of mine were less complex. The wizard that was also my dog (because it wasn't just an illusion, the onesie had turned a wizard into my dog) looked up at her and smiled.

It was three years later that we decided to mark our Silver Day.

Honestly, I'd been ready sooner, but Elspeth put it off. This made me sad, at first. Your Silver Day is when you mark the transition from Friend to Best Friend or Dear One. I thought, for a while, that she didn't feel the same way about me. Which would have been fine! But … sad.

"It's just that I've been having such bad dreams recently," she told me, eventually, when she was ready to let the words unburden her tongue. "I don't want to make you go through that."

I said some stupid stuff about how it wouldn't be 'putting me through' anything. About how I was sure it wouldn't be that bad and how it'd be better if we dreamed it together. A nightmare shared is a nightmare halved, after all.

She didn't talk to me for a while after that.

I thought about it for a while. Then I thought about it some more. I slowly rolled the words round my brain and then rolled them round my mouth, testing the shape and the flavour of them.

When they finally felt right, I said:

"So … I know it's not going to be okay. I know that sharing something awful with me won't make it *better*. I know that sharing it might actually make it worse, because you'll be more scared and more vulnerable. It won't be halved. But it will be *shared*. And even if it's scary and even if it hurts – even if it's scarier and hurts more – that sharing is still important. But I understand, I think, why you might not be ready. Because letting someone into the secret bits of you means they can hurt you and they can get hurt. But, like, when you're ready … I'd like to do it still. I'd like to know there's a bit of you in the secret places of me and the other way round, too. It might not make the nightmares better, but it might make us happier when we wake up. That's what I think at least. What do you think?"

And after I said that, Elspeth smiled, and we talked some more. We talked a *lot* more.

A year later, we were finally ready and we had our Silver Day and celebrated each other as close, dear, and darling friends.

She took three silver earrings and put two in the helix of my left ear and one in my right.

I took a small silver chain and fastened it around her ankle.

We celebrated our Salt Day the next day, which was unexpected. Often you don't get a Salt Day. Often you don't need one.

Perhaps it's a bad sign that our first Silver Dream was one that needed to be scrubbed with salt. But it was bad. Bad enough we both woke up shaking and screaming and sweating.

I called Elspeth and asked: "Is this what it's like? Is this what it's like every night for you?"

And she said no. She said it had been worse.

But she didn't shy away. She trusted me even more. I was glad we'd taken our time.

I took the next flight over. And when I arrived, she put the salt in my hand, and I washed her hair and rubbed the salt into her temples and her scalp where I could feel the traces of the previous night's dream.

It was a struggle. It didn't go easy. But we fought it off, together.

Now we neither of us remember what that dream was.

Now we are Ribbon Friends, Silver Friends and Salt Friends. We share our dreams every night and often they are still nightmares. It doesn't get easier.

But every morning we wake up cradling the ribbon and the silver that bind us. And we know we aren't alone.

And that's something. It is certainly something.

And we always have the salt bond to call on … if we ever need it again.

49.

Tough

A friend sometimes tells me
I'm too tough on the person
I once was.

And I will admit, he had some highlights.

He had compasses for eyes
Always ready for adventure
Hand up to high five the tide
As it sent legs and needle tumbling.

He had ink on his fingers
And on his tongue
Ready to spit at predators from his always-at-hand notebook.

He had a collection of interesting bruises.

He had a cartographer's ear
He listened until he had you mapped
And sometimes got lost there.
He had terrible balance.

He had compasses for eyes
Always knew where his north was

But he did not always reach it.

He was unkind
He was unthinking
He did not know the lines
That marked what was his
And what belonged to other people.

Sometimes his eyes lost the compass
But remembered the needles.

And perhaps I dwell on this
Because he made the call
To transform himself into someone
More like me.

He was already learning the parts of him
He wanted to leave in the past.
He was marking on his skin
With little X's
The places we buried
Anger
Entitlement
Gender.

I'm not the person I want to be yet
I never will be

But I am trying to be grateful to the boy
Who set the course
That got the creature I am this far.

50.

Toothbrush

WHEN ALEX REALISED their home was not a place they could go back to, they offered up a silent prayer.

They knew, deep down, that prayers like this could be dangerous. There were so many gods out there listening, both old and new, big and small, benevolent and wicked. If a god with a twist of mischief in their smile answered your prayer, there would be a sting in the tail that could make your life a misery.

Or worse: it could make your life a *story*.

But Alex was tired. Exhausted. They were the kind of weary that turns your thoughts to stones sinking in deep and murky water, and turns feelings into the distant sound of rushing waves.

So, when the thought that warned them about inviting such 'interesting times' entered their brain, they simply noticed it but let it sink unheard into the depths of Not Right Now. And they prayed their prayer.

A short while later, they were walking through the city streets when the streetlamps flickered. No... it was too regular and defined to be called a flicker, this felt more like the city had *winked* at them.

Their phone vibrated in their pocket. This was odd, as they were sure the battery had died. They checked it and found it resurrected, at 3% power. The vibration was a text from a friend, offering them a sofa to sleep on – it included a link to a mapping app called Mercury. Alex didn't recognise the app, but their phone seemed to already have it installed. They opened it and a glowing thread unfolded on their phone's half-bright screen.

The UI was elegant and gorgeous, made up of simple silver lines that spread out like paintbrush strokes over the night grey of the cityscape.

They followed the quicksilver path it laid out and, as they walked, the city sang them a comforting wordless song of distant trains and electric hums.

When they arrived at their friend's flat, Alex took a bottle of water and a granola bar from their bag. Without really thinking about why, they poured a mouthful of water out onto the porch, at the top of the final step. Then they broke off a small chunk of granola and laid it carefully down, too.

Alex knocked on the door. Their friend was surprised to see them and didn't recall sending Alex any texts that evening, but did still offer Alex a couch to sleep on. The friend asked no questions, but offered many hugs, and Alex even accepted one (they felt like anything more than a single, gentle embrace might break their paper-thin bones).

That night, Alex went to the bathroom to wash before bed and was surprised to find a new toothbrush waiting for them on the sink. It was one of those cheap plastic ones you might find in a hostel – barely better than scrubbing your teeth with your finger. But, for a moment, Alex was sure that the bristles glowed a soft gold.

Alex's eyes whipped up at the gentle sound of a throat clearing, scanning for danger, to find a warm and friendly face staring back at them from the mirror with a lopsided smile.

He was not one of Alex's gods, but Alex still knew him.

"Hey kid," said Hephaestus. "I know it's not much, but I made it for you."

Alex picked up the toothbrush and smiled cautiously back.

"Thanks. I, uh, don't mean to sound ungrateful… but I didn't think looking after waifs and strays was your jam."

"Oh, it's not what I'm best known for." He spoke with the steady cadence of a hammer ringing out on hot metal. "But I have a fondness for those who find themselves lost. If you have no hearth to call your own, sometimes a forge will do the job for a while."

"Um. Thanks." Alex felt something catch in their throat. "For this. The directions, the words, and the… the toothbrush."

"Well, thank *you* for the drink and the snack. Such a kind offering definitely buys you clean teeth, at least." He winked and, as he did, the light in the bathroom flickered. "And besides, creating things that are dearly needed … that *is* what I'm known for. You take care now."

With that, the face in the mirror dissolved into a shower

of fiery sparks.

Alex paused for a while – brain blank, tears beginning to well in their eyes.

Then, remembering the toothbrush was still in their hand, they began to clean their teeth. And for the first time that night, Alex began to feel human again.

51.

Seed Energy

WHEN I THINK about what kind of 'energy' you have, I find myself wanting to talk about myself. I apologise for my inevitable solipsism, but if you bear with me this tale may still bear fruit.

When I was thirteen, I buried a story in the forest.

It was the first story I'd ever written that I wasn't happy with. It was a great rambling thing, spread out across innumerable notebooks in crowded, excitable handwriting.

It was a map of where I had been, a cartography made of tears and recycled fairy tales and interesting leaves. It was written and overwritten and crossed out and corrected with post-its and notes written on receipts. It was a hot, hot mess.

Like me.

And being a hot mess of a teenager, I decided the only thing to do with this story was to bury it so no-one would ever find it. I dug a hole beneath the stump of an oak tree that had been struck by lightning and I placed the many notebooks in the hole and covered them up with dirt and ash.

I did this very solemnly, for killing your creations is a serious business.

Some years later, I was walking through the forest. I had almost forgotten the story by then. When I did remember it, I thought of it sadly, for I had come to think of that sprawling story like an old friend I had drifted apart from. But now, perhaps, I was in a position to offer them a tad more grace, and to find a little love for their messy, overwhelmed and all-at-once self.

And that is when I came across the Story Buds. There was a small bush of them, growing in scrawled black and white balls around thin black twigs. At first I thought they were cotton, but for the colour, which was creamier than cotton. And the writing of course.

Reading the writing on the buds, the stories they told (small things so far, and clearly unfinished) felt familiar, but not overly so. They were like a friend of a friend that you've seen pictures of and always thought looked kind of cool. They were like a distant cousin whom your aunts always told you had a touch of the fae about them and warned you to stay away from.

Intrigued, and remembering again my old story, I dug in the ground beneath the bush.

And there I found what was left of my notebooks, a mush of ink and dirt and paper, from which sprouted strange watercolour mushrooms and glowing verse-covered worms and the roots of the Story Buds.

The mess of it smelled of muddy decay and moss, cut across with a clean scent of cotton and hot, fresh-printed ink.

I stared at it, transfixed by this gruesome, beautiful sight. The earth was eating up the old stories and breaking them down to their constituent parts.

I carried some of the Buds home with me. One of my beloveds took one look at it and set to work with it on an old spinning wheel they'd been playing around with. Then a very old friend, who had recently been learning how to weave, began to turn it into scarves and coats.

Put all together, the Story Buds made garments of a shimmering quality, like a sandy riverbed obscured by ink-scrawled currents. Put together like this, the stories were finally finished; things of rare, rich strangeness.

They were quite popular for a time; we took great pleasure in matching each customer to the right garment and the right story for them. For there was always something in these tales wherein a reader could see themselves, despite their otherworldly, alien magic.

No. Not despite. *Because* of the magic and blood and fierceness, there was always something familiar in them.

And when I think of that mangled seed of rot and words, from which all of that sprang... I think of you.

I'm not saying you are mush and fungus and the kind of energy that devours dead things (though that would be pretty cool, too).

I'm saying you have growth energy. Resurrection energy. Phoenix energy. You have the energy that feasts on old stories that would chew us up, and turn them into *ours*.

52.

Where The Light Gets Out

Z ED WAS STANDING on the space station's observation deck; the window curved round above and below, making it seem like they floated amid the glittering cosmos. They let their head hang over the railing, watching their tears sparkle like crystals falling through the air to smash on the thick glass beneath.

Since Zed had arrived, things had been so busy – so many people there for the collision – that they barely had time to breathe, let alone cry. But it was Iate in the shift cycle by then, so observation was mostly deserted.

As the tears spread, they began to blur out the galaxies in the distance. Zed didn't smile, but it brought them some small satisfaction to think that their sadness was strong enough to wash away solar systems.

"You know there are stars in your tears?"

Rook had always been a bit of a lurker. Something about them was always a little too soft, a little too inwards to be noticed.

"Are you being poetic again?" Zed didn't make any move

to wipe away the moisture on their cheeks. There was no hiding from Rook anyway – they had lurked through many of Zed's tears and injuries. They knew all of each other's scars and ugly faces.

"No. Just descriptive. The stars, they're reflected in your tears. They contain suns."

Zed huffed and wiped a strand of bright silver hair out of their eyes. It was something akin to watching a polar bear wrinkle its nose: catching a moment where something wild and fierce is suddenly disarmed.

"No. They extinguish them."

It sounded stupid, said out loud. But Rook looked down at the tears on the concave window, then Rook looked at Zed and said:

"An astrological flood. Moses would be proud."

"Your Earth history is shit. Moses didn't make the flood. God did, for humanity had grown wicked."

Rook looked away, a little sadly. They both stared out of the window for a moment. From the right angle, they could see each other reflected in the blurred glass. Zed all ursine hulk and big wide eyes, Rook like a lightning bolt streaked in black velvet.

"You know they used to think the binary stars of this system were gods?" Rook's voice was quiet as always, but held the threat of an edge beneath the silk. "Some still do, I suppose, in a more metaphorical way."

"Yeah?"

"Yes. Gods that were always chasing each other across the sky."

Zed turned. Rook mirrored them without thinking. Zed looked Rook in the eye; Rook's eyes were bloodshot as theirs, but they often were. It didn't always mean tears, it could just mean their implants were acting up.

"Were they mad at each other?" Zed asked, quietly. But even Zed's whispers filled the room.

"Stories differ. Sometimes they hated each other. Other times they were in love. Sometimes both."

"So what does it mean that their two gods are about to crash into each other?"

Rook smiled and rubbed their nose. Adjusting glasses that hadn't been there for years. "Fucked if I know."

"Maybe they finally caught up and will destroy each other?" Zed's voice wasn't bitter, not really. It almost sounded like they envied those gods… well, maybe it did sound a *little* bitter.

"Or maybe they're finally going to get to embrace." Rook let the little finger of their left hand rest against the little finger of Zed's right. A touch so light it could have been accidental. A question was being asked.

"And the kilonova?"

Rook let a little sharpness into their smile. "Well, they love each other so *fiercely*…"

Zed took Rook's hand in their own. They turned to watch the stars, hand in hand.

"So do you think it'll be like watching gods clash? When they collide?" asked Zed.

"Honestly," Rook let the words roll around their mouth, chewing them over a little. "I was thinking about the cracks.

These two stars – these twins, old as ever – are about to smash each other to pieces." Rook held up both their hands to gently trace the slow (but getting faster) spiral orbit of the two nearest stars. "So hard the walls of the universe will tremble. The ending of these two things will be so powerful it will make *maths* shake."

They made a ka-pow sound, miming an explosion using both their hands.

"But it's not an end. Not really. It's an ignition."

Rook pointed to the Cradle Engine, the vast machine that encircled the system in a mess of mile-wide circuits and skyscraper high hard-light proboscis. Its chrome tendrils snaked around the ever shrinking orbit of the stars.

"The nova – the kilonova, sorry – we're going to use it to kick-start that monster. And that beast will spread its tentacles out through the gaps this impact leaves. Through the spaces they shake in the numbers. These stars – these gods – they're going to crack open not just each other, but *reality*. And we had the audacity to look at two deities about to end each other and say: we can *use that*. Have you been to see the demo yet? Have you seen the Stellar Tunnels? They look like gold. They look like light."

They stroked a strand of silver hair behind Zed's ear as they continued. "Then, when the dusters have swept up all the gold and platinum – the precious metals these two gods create when they finally kiss – we'll use it to make more circuits. To expand the system. The collision of these giants creates the materials for their resurrection."

Zed slid an arm around Rook's waist and the two of them

stood there, connected (albeit a tad lopsided, thanks to their differing heights).

"And we'll use that to fill the galaxies with more Tunnels. With more light." Rook finished.

Zed thought for a moment, then they gave a little gasp.

"We're filling the cracks in the universe with gold," they said.

"Yes," said Rook.

"Cohen wasn't quite right, though."

"Leonard? How so?"

"The cracks aren't where the light gets in."

"No?"

Zed reached out with one hand as if to touch the binary stars in front of them. "All the light, it's coming from these two. It's the gift that they'll give us."

"A gift." Rook sometimes had a way of saying words like they were appreciating their flavour.

"It's not where the light gets *in*."

Zed smiled at Rook. They were both smiling. They were both crying. There were stars in their tears.

"The crack in everything… that's where the light gets *out*."

Dear Reader

Thank you for reading *Hopefully Ever After*. If you enjoyed this book (or even if you didn't) please consider leaving a star rating or review online. Your feedback is important, and will help other readers who find the book decide whether to read it, too.

Acknowledgements

So here we are. Another collection finished; 52 stories tied together with glue and ink and (of course) hope.

The theme of this one is near and dear to me (as I imagine it is to you, if you're reading this). After all, the whole reason I started writing these 'strange little stories' was to bring a little light to the grey days of some of my favourite people. Over time, I wrote more and the pool of people I wrote for expanded. And now that includes you! Please know that *you* are now one of my favourite people and I dearly wish that you have found in these words a little spark of hope.

If so, please take that spark away with you. Feed it. Plant it in the ground, perhaps. Let it grow. Make something out of it. Gird yourself with it. Hope is a verb, just like create, resist, trespass, survive, love, and give. And also mischief (if you try hard enough).

I owe gratitude to many, but I will start with Sara and Inspired Quill. Your belief in my writing, your eagle-eyed editing, and your values as a publisher are massively appreciated. It is a delight to be part of the IQ family. A particular thanks for your patience with my flakiness, and for always giving me a reason to write more and to write better.

Thanks, too, to Venetia who designed the cover for this book, and indeed for my previous two. Your work is astonishing – capturing not just the soul of each collection, but also sitting together beautifully as a trio: day, night and dusk/dawn.

Though I do not know them personally, a big thank you to Alexandra Rowland who coined the term 'hopepunk' and whose writing on that genre struck a chord that continues to resonate with me clearly, powerfully and complexly.

To my partners – Zan, Theo and Robin L – I appreciate you bearing with me as I occasionally disappear into my various creative endeavours. And more than that, I appreciate your company, your inspiration, protection and insight. There is a piece of each of you in me and in this book, and both are richer because of it. Please know also that my gratitude will not in any way stop me being an *utter nuisance* in your direction; you have been warned (not that you needed to be).

To everyone who inspired one of the stories in this book: big love and bigger appreciation. Miranda, Aquarion, Amy, Peter, Oliver, Lucy, Paul, Simara, Theo, Jesse, Dana, Becca, Olwen, Zan, Dorian, Dre, Tori, and Robin G: thank you for all you've done for me and for the world around you.

A thorough thanking also to my family, to mum and dad, to my sisters, and to all the Websters, the Boustreds, the Gregorys, and all the rest. It is your fault (and credit) that I am the way I am.

And to my chosen family: the musketeers, the OxBlob, the larpers, writers, thesps, wrestlers, roller derby players, CrossFitters and assorted other nerds/jocks/vagabonds. Thanks and blame also go unto thee. It is to your credit (and fault) that I am still here, happy, healthy and *like this*.

Shamelessly, I also thank my weekly TTRPG game (and all the games gone by); it is a deep magic to be able to practice hope with you every week.

And finally, of course, big love and thanks for Ayrton. 'She of light'. You, Paul and Rowan are ever a source of joy and hope – a lighthouse across stormy seas.

About the Author

James is an inveterate scribbler of poetry and prose who can most reliably be found writing weird little stories online, on a stage somewhere, doing something that can only be described as 'proclaiming'.

As a poet, he's won multiple slams, performed up and down the UK (mainly down) and written two full-length spoken word theatre shows (*50 Shades of Webster* and *Poor Life Choices*) that he's performed at various festivals and even one sci-fi convention.

When not performing, e's had poetry published in a couple of anthologies, but most often publishes microfiction and flash fiction on es Tumblr, Strange Little Stories.

James likes his stories the same way he likes his friends/partners: somewhat surprising, perfectly formed and weird as hell.

Find the author via their website:
strangelittlestories.tumblr.com
Or on socials: @StrangeLittleStories

More From This Author

Heroine Chic

"I am the girl the Lost Boys lost."

Queens and Scoundrels. Witches and Rebels. Grifters and Goddesses. These are stories about heroines.

From prolific poet and writer James Webster, featuring 52 very short stories, *Heroine Chic* is a celebration of the heroine's place at the heart of science fiction, fantasy, and reality. Told with humour, daring, and gorgeous lyricism, these are tales of magic, love, adventure, SCIENCE! and much more.

Available from all major online and offline outlets.

Monstrous Ink

"I saw a fury on the street today."

Talons and teeth. Lairs and labyrinths. Those beasts we fear and those we secretly admire. These are stories about monsters.

Featuring 52 very short stories, Monstrous Ink is a deep-dive into the murky waters of monster-dom from which so many of our most beloved sci-fi and fantasy stories came.

Told with sharp insight, spiky humour, and spine-tingling atmosphere, these tales explore what it means to be a monster and the power of reclaiming what (we fear) is monstrous inside ourselves.

Available from all major online and offline outlets.

9 781913 117290